MARIAN BABSON

Murder, Murder, Little Star

WALKER AND COMPANY ✸ NEW YORK

- M- 4/80 East. 664

© William Collins Sons & Co Ltd 1977

All rights reserved. No part of this book may
be reproduced or transmitted in any form or by
any means, electric or mechanical, including
photocopying, recording, or by any information
storage and retrieval system, without permission
in writing from the Publisher.

All the characters and events portrayed in this
story are fictitious.

First published in the United States of America
in 1980 by the Walker Publishing Company, Inc.

ISBN: 0-8027-5416-3

Library of Congress Catalog Card Number: 79-91254

Printed in the United States of America

10 9 8 7 6 5 4 3 2 1

CHAPTER I

There was really, Frances Armitage thought complacently, a lot of nonsense talked about the difficulty of re-entering the employment market. The man across the desk from her was practically pleading with her to accept the job.

'Are you certain you really want *me*? There are so many other applicants out there – ' She indicated the reception room outside, which was crowded with younger, and possibly more suitable, women. 'You haven't seen half of them yet – '

'Oh yes, I have, Mrs Armitage.' Mr Herkimer fixed her with a desperate gaze, obviously determined to break down resistance. 'I've seen *all* of them a hundred – no, a thousand – times before. You're different.'

'But I thought you might want someone nearer her own age, someone with the same interests – '

'Oh, they've got those, all right. That's what's the matter with them. Listen – ' Mr Herkimer leaned forward intently. 'I've been through all this before, remember. Believe me, I know. I hire one of them bints and next thing I know, she's trying to elbow the star right off the screen and grab a piece of the action for herself. They're all alike. That's why I want you. Let's say another five pounds a week, okay?'

'Well, yes,' Frances Armitage said faintly. 'But I really thought – '

'Listen.' Mr Herkimer raked her with an assessing

glance. 'If you didn't think you'd get this job, why did you want to apply for it in the first place?'

Actually, to try to get back into the swing of going for interviews again, but one could hardly admit that. To do so would be to betray the lack of self-confidence that had led her to expect weeks, perhaps months, of hopeless knocking on Personnel Department doors before finding a firm willing to hire her. Probably as one of the filing clerks her supercilious daughter-in-law assured her that industry could always use.

'You're quite right.' She sat straighter and attempted to emulate Mr Herkimer's crispness. 'It's just that I was a bit daunted by the sight of so much competition – ' (All those flawlessly lacquered young girls who so obviously knew their way around this world which was strange to her.)

'No competition at all.' Mr Herkimer dismissed the bevy of beauties outside with a wave of his hand. 'You got everything we want.'

'Well, I hope so – '

'You got no ties – ' Mr Herkimer ticked off the advantages she offered. 'You understand kids – you've brought up two of your own. You can drive. You're free to travel.' He summed up. 'We're gonna enjoy working together.' He stood up. The interview appeared to be at an end.

'I certainly hope so, Mr Herkimer.'

'Call me Herkie. Everybody does.' He escorted her to the door, looking rather surprised at himself. 'And I'll see you at Heathrow in the morning.'

Really, she thought as she left, it had all been so simple. With one interview and a minimum of effort, she had landed the first job she had applied for.

Furthermore, it was a job that would quite fairly be rated in the glamour category, and the salary offered had been generous even before Mr Herkimer had raised it. It had all been so beautifully simple.

If she had been wiser in the ways of the employment world, that alone would have made her suspicious.

CHAPTER II

After Roger Armitage's sudden death in a laboratory explosion six years ago, Frances had thrown herself into a phase of 'living for the children'. Insurance money and a subsequent *ex gratia* payment from the laboratory, who denied all responsibility for the accident while admitting to a certain combination of unfortunate circumstances leading up to it, had made it unnecessary for her to go out to work. Apart from which, Simon and Rosemary had been teenagers and it had seemed more important to look after them.

But children grow up so quickly. Simon had married just over a year ago. (Much too young at twenty-two, but she had been eighteen when she had married, so what could she say?) Then it had been time for Rosemary to start at university, with all the attendant flurry of preparations, planning and shopping. It was not until the train actually pulled out, leaving Frances still waving from the platform, that the dismal let-down of anti-climax had swamped her and she had returned home alone and cried.

So, there it was: crisis time. '*So* nice for you to have the house all to yourself,' her friends had said cheerfully. (From the depths of houses crowded with life and action.) '*So* lovely to have your time to yourself again.'

Time. Endless time to sit and contemplate the wasteland surrounding her. Time to take stock – and to realize just how much time she had.

At forty-two, she was far too young and energetic to be able to close up her life and occupy herself with a house and a garden. Nor could she see herself settling down to a future of cooing over grandchildren – even had Amanda shown signs of being willing to provide any within the next decade, or of being the sort of mother who might allow a grandmother within doting distance oftener than Christmas and Easter.

There was always charity work, but that somehow seemed rather unsatisfactory. There were too many professionals available these days who could do the job more competently and might (shades of Amanda) treat amateur volunteers with thinly-veiled impatience and contempt. Also, and perhaps more importantly, there were Amanda's insinuations that one was paid what one was worth – and that people who took jobs for which they did not receive payment had found their correct level and should, therefore, be left at that level.

However, another point on which she was determined was that she was not going to devolve into the sort of woman who made a career out of warring with her daughter-in-law. Simon must work out his own problems – although, to be fair, he seemed quite happy in his marriage. All the more reason for his mother not to turn into an interfering in-law.

Obviously, the answer was to find a job. Or to 're-enter the employment market', as Amanda's sociology textbooks phrased it. Her self-assurance was not strengthened by the realization that she could hardly have been deemed to have ever 'entered' it in the first place.

However, the advertisement in that morning's *Times* had seemed as good a place to start as any; perhaps better than most since it called for a telephoned response which would save her the difficult task of drafting a letter of application.

She had been somewhat taken aback by the cordial invitation to come for an interview that afternoon. And now, amazingly, the job was hers. It had all happened so fast that she had not had time to sort out her feelings properly yet.

On the whole, she was pleased. Even though Simon and Amanda were coming over for dinner tonight to say goodbye to Rosemary, who was going off in the morning for a month's working holiday with friends in France, and her own long afternoon in town meant that the menu she had originally planned would have to be abandoned. Tonight, *she* would be the one serving frozen food with fulsomely false apologies.

That didn't displease her, either.

'I'm sorry about that, darling,' Frances said, as she saw Simon stab at a limp prawn with an expression of dismayed incredulity. (He had been trained into acceptance of this state of things from his wife, but he expected better from his mother.)

'It doesn't matter,' Simon said despondently. Rosemary still appeared to be in a state of mild shock; she had never had to accustom herself to family meals like this, particularly for a farewell dinner.

'Of course it doesn't.' Amanda alone was telling the

truth, seeing nothing untoward about the meal, and anxious to finish it and get back to her work. (It was unthinkable that she should face a boring evening with her in-laws without bringing along a bulwark of work. And market research, it seemed, required a constant stream of reports interpreting what the public actually meant when it answered designated questions.)

'I knew *you'd* understand.' Frances beamed a totally insincere smile at her daughter-in-law. 'We working women must stick together, mustn't we?'

'Working?' Amanda's head snapped up abruptly.

'I start in the morning,' Frances said complacently. 'So I'm afraid that's why things have been rather rushed tonight.'

'Mother – what?' Simon stared at her.

'Mother – when?' Rosemary looked blank.

'Mother – *how*?' One could always depend on Amanda for the tactless, if not the downright insulting.

'I answered an advertisement in *The Times* this morning,' Frances said. 'I went for the interview this afternoon, and I start work in the morning.'

'But you're not qualified for anything,' Amanda gasped.

'They seemed to feel I had all the qualifications they needed.' Frances smiled at Simon and Rosemary, then frowned as a new thought occurred to her.

'I'm afraid, Rosemary,' she said, 'you'll have to get a taxi to the station in the morning. I'll need the car to get to Heathrow by nine.'

'You're *not* leaving the country?' Having assimilated the basic fact, Simon now appeared ready to believe anything.

'No, dear, but I have to link up with the Unit.

They're arriving on the first flight.'

'What Unit?' Amanda asked suspiciously, something in her mother-in-law's attitude alerting her to the fact that she was not going to relish the answer.

'The Film Unit.' The line was so sensational one could afford to throw it away. 'More rice?' she enquired innocently.

'Films?' Rosemary perked up, foreseeing unexpected status about to be conferred by having a mother in the media.

'What *sort* of films?' Amanda managed to convey the impression that anyone so ill-equipped to cope with the world as her mother-in-law would unfailingly find that she had become involved in blue movies and they would all wind up in the Sunday Sensationals to the immediate destruction of their reputations and burgeoning careers.

'Oh, quite respectable, I assure you.' Frances allowed a moment for the suspense to build. (Perhaps Mr Herkimer had been wrong about her, perhaps she had unsuspected dramatic longings.) 'Herkimer-Torrington Productions, in fact.'

'Herkimer-Torrington!' Even Amanda couldn't try to pretend that she had never heard of *them*. 'But they're a major studio. They're important.'

'So I understand.'

'You don't think Mother would settle for anything less than the best!' Rosemary said loyally, making it sound as though Frances had had a choice of any studio she would deign to work for.

Simon just whistled.

'But – ' Amanda still struggled for comprehension – 'what are you going to *do* for them? I mean, what *can* you do? In films?' She spoke as though she still cherished a forlorn hope that the answer might be 'Tea lady'.

'Well, they tell me – ' She wasn't feigning modesty, it was just that the incredulous feeling that had been coming and going all afternoon swept over her again. 'They say I'll be chaperone and sort of secretary to the star.'

'But you can't even type!' Amanda wailed. 'Let alone take shorthand.'

'Oh, I shouldn't think she'll be dictating many letters,' Frances said. 'She's only ten years old. It's Twinkle, you know.'

'Twinkle!' Amanda knew. In a series of films about lovable children, Twinkle had made her mark on the Great British Public quite as indelibly as she had on the Great American Public. People who had not been to any film in years that wasn't pretentious foreign soft-porn had heard of Twinkle.

'It's just glorified child-minding, I expect,' Frances tried to comfort the stricken Amanda. 'Her mother has been ill recently, I gather, and they want a sort of substitute to help with the long tedious hours at the Studio.'

'Studio?' Amanda rallied, becoming more like her old self. 'I certainly think you might have found something closer to home – something more suitable.' She even found a grievance. 'If I'd known you were *serious* about working, I could have got you something in market research.'

'Oh, yes?' That was too much. It was the first time such an offer had ever been made, although Frances had 'seriously' mentioned going to work on several occasions. '*Do* tell us about your latest project, dear. Something to do with housewives and fish fingers, isn't it?'

Routed, Amanda declared an early evening due to pressure of work and departed with Simon a good hour and a half earlier than Frances had dared hope.

CHAPTER III

Heathrow, by dawn's early light, was a futuristic city peopled by ghosts obviously regretting their past lives, especially the one they had led last night. Frances parked the car and marched purposefully past grey-faced automatons who were carrying, wheeling or just slumped over pieces of luggage. Other uniformed automatons drifted dreamlike along shining corridors or shuffled aimlessly through stacks of paper at desks. An occasional bright-faced, alert specimen seemed to act only as a focus for resentment; Frances was aware of vague emanations of hostility from underwater groups as she passed them.

'Over here!' Mr Herkimer hailed her and waved her onwards. 'We want Gate 12 – that's where our Red-eye Flight comes in.'

'Red-eye?' It couldn't be a new airline, could it? Perhaps something to do with American Redskins.

'Wait'll you see them. Then you'll know why we call it that. Up all night, what do you expect? Who can sleep? Except Morris, that is?'

Racing across the terminal with Mr Herkimer, already slightly out of breath, Frances became aware of an unnerving swishing sound following after them. She turned to see two uniformed attendants scurrying behind them, pushing empty wheelchairs. They increased their speed when Mr Herkimer increased his speed, swerved when he swerved, slowed when he slowed. There was no escaping them; they were definitely with Mr Herkimer. For the first time, Frances was conscious of a feeling of foreboding.

'Mr Herkimer –' she said breathlessly, 'Mr Herkimer, what are those – ?'

'Herkie!' he snapped over his shoulder. 'I told you. Call me Herkie. Everybody does.' Putting on a fresh burst of speed, he outdistanced her.

'Herkie –' she gasped, catching up. Gate 12 loomed just ahead of them.

'This way!' He snatched at her elbow and propelled her along. 'We've got permission to go straight through. On accounta *them*.' He jerked his thumb backwards and when Frances turned around, she saw that several reporters and cameramen had joined the wheelchair men, leaving her uncertain which ones Mr Herkimer was referring to.

'Mr – Herkie –' She plucked at his sleeve. 'Is there anything wrong?' She had a sudden vision of a heap of crumpled wreckage on a runway. 'Has something happened?'

'You mean *them*?' He shook his head. 'Naw, that's okay. They're just here to take Morris to the ambulance.'

'Ambulance?'

'Take it easy, will you?' He slowed a little, going through the gate. 'I told you there's nothing wrong. It's only Morris. Morris Moskva – greatest scriptwriter you ever saw, but he can't stand planes. Morrie hasn't made a vertical flight in twenty years. He figures, if the plane crashes, he don't want to know about it. So we wheel him on at one end and wheel him off at the other. Then we just throw him on a bed in the hotel until he sleeps off the pills. After that, he's ready to work. Greatest scriptwriter you ever saw – when he's conscious, that is.'

'Yes, but – ' Frances was only partly mollified. 'But does it take *two* wheelchairs to carry him?'

'Oh, yeah, well – ' Up ahead, a group of people who could only be called a motley crew were gathered around an Immigration Desk. Mr Herkimer suddenly seemed less anxious to join them than he had been. 'Well, I'll tell you. Sometimes Laurenda isn't always feeling so good. Twinkle's mother, you know? So the second wheelchair is a sort of back-up operation. Just in case she needs it.'

'I see,' Frances said. Her uneasiness increased.

'Well . . .' Mr Herkimer gave a deep sigh. His attention appeared to be centred on a midget in a fur coat and dark glasses. 'We gotta get with it, I suppose.' He put on a fresh burst of speed and reached the Immigration Desk just as the Press converged on it.

'Here you are – ' The Immigration Officer was just finishing, he extended a slim grey passport to the over-dressed midget. 'Welcome to England, Miss Tilling – '

'What was that name –?' one of the newsmen began.

'Twinkle!' Mr Herkimer swooped on the midget, enveloping her in an embrace she did not appear to relish. 'This is Twinkle – our ten-year-old star. Twinkle – that's the only name she's got. Twinkle – like in star.'

Behind him, the Immigration man flipped open the passport again for another look. With a flick of an eyebrow and a grin he didn't bother to conceal, he then passed it to the pallid-faced woman who held her hand out. '*Mrs* Tilling,' he murmured.

Laurenda Tilling – Twinkle's mother – took the passport and her own passport without acknowledging the smile. Her attention seemed concentrated on her daughter – or perhaps on the Press people surrounding Twinkle.

From the background, a uniformed airline stewardess with an armload of fur coats, airline bags and assorted impedimenta, moved forward slowly. Her regulation smile seemed less plastic than carven granite. Unerringly, she zeroed-in on Frances.

'You're part of the London end?' she enquired tonelessly.

'This is our Frances – ' Mr Herkimer contrived to kiss Laurenda Tilling on one cheek, introduce Frances, pat Twinkle on the head, wave the stewardess beyond the Immigration barrier and direct one wheelchair plus attendant towards the plane – all at the same moment. 'Frances Armitage. I promise you, Laurenda, she's a doll. You won't have a problem in the world while she's around. She'll take care of everything.'

Laurenda Tilling waved a limp hand in her direction. Twinkle ignored her. The stewardess advanced mechanically and began unloading her burdens into Frances's unresisting arms.

Flashbulbs were popping off all around them. Blinking through an after-image of coloured flashes, Frances saw Twinkle round on a photographer who had been staring at her.

'What's the matter?' Twinkle demanded. 'Haven't you ever seen sable before?'

'Not on anyone under forty,' the photographer mumbled.

'Twinkle, darling – ' Mr Herkimer, too, had heard the exchange and swooped on her. He pressed her to his capacious abdomen, one hand covering her mouth, and patted her head again with his other hand.

'Such a long journey – ' he said to the journalists – 'for such a little girl. She's tired, but she's delighted to be here in London and looking forward to making this film with the cream of the English theatre as her co-stars – Ouch!'

'Supporting players,' Twinkle said coldly. Mr Herkimer was nursing his hand, on which a semi-circle of sharp indentations was clearly visible.

'I hope he's getting a rabies shot,' the photographer said with concern.

'What do you think of London, Twinkle?' a journalist asked.

'It's a place.' Twinkle shrugged.

'Jet lag!' Mr Herkimer burst in. 'She's only ten years old and she's exhausted. It's been an all-night flight, remember. Later on, we'll call a Press Conference. She'll answer all your questions then.'

The stewardess finished transferring her burdens and looked at Frances curiously. 'You're actually joining this circus?' she asked.

'I've already joined,' Frances said.

The wheelchair swished past on its return journey, a massive shape huddled in it, swathed in a rumpled blanket; the head was tilted forward, face buried in the blanket. Only a patch of curiously grey skin was visible on the back of his head.

'Here!' The sight seemed to inspire Mr Herkimer. 'Over here!' He beckoned frantically to the second wheelchair and attendant.

Silently, Frances and the stewardess watched as Laurenda Tilling sank into the wheelchair, eyes closed, looking paler than ever. Twinkle, the limelight abruptly wrenched away from her, hovered in the background, abruptly looking as unhappy and miserable as any ten-year-old whose mother was on the verge of inexplicable collapse.

Instinctively, Frances moved forward. Mr Herkimer looked up and reached out to grasp her arm. 'Yes. Here, Fran, here,' he ordered. 'Take Laurenda to the hotel. And look after her. . . . And Twinkle, too,' he added as an afterthought.

Before she could do so, another hand gripped her other arm. She turned back to face the stewardess, who looked not only worried, but faintly guilty.

'Here – ' The stewardess pushed a small vial of capsules at her. 'You'd better take these. You're going to need them. It's all right,' she added, as she saw the uneasy expression flit across Frances's face. 'They're only tranquillizers.'

'But – ' Frances felt her fingers close over the vial as though it were a straw and she were drowning. 'Who are they for?' She looked from one wheelchair to the other, to Twinkle, even to Mr Herkimer.

'Are you kidding?' The stewardess patted her hand and began to edge away, relief emanating from every fibre of her being. 'They're for *you*. Who else? Believe me, dearie, you're gonna need them!'

CHAPTER IV

The hotel suite was larger than most flats. Since the others seemed to take this luxury for granted, Frances tried to look as though she too were accustomed to it.

'It looks like a funeral.' Twinkle curled her lips. 'All those lousy flowers.'

'Don't say things like that!' Still slumped in her wheelchair, Laurenda raised her head. 'Don't talk about funerals. It's unlucky.'

'Where do you want these?' A bellboy pushed a trolley laden with luggage through the doorway and came to a halt behind the wheelchair.

'Luck-schmuck!' Twinkle shrugged and turned away. Laurenda fumbled ineffectively with the wheels of the chair, as though she would follow her, then gave up and slumped back in the chair, closing her eyes.

Without a backward glance, Twinkle marched into the sitting-room, leaving the others in the reception hall.

Mr Herkimer had stopped downstairs at the porter's desk on some errand on his own. Two unidentified people, a man and a woman, had come up to the suite – Frances vaguely remembered them from the airport – but seemed to have lost interest in the proceedings at a fairly early stage and had wandered off to explore.

Another wheelchair, bearing the still-unconscious mountain that was Morris Moskva, pulled up behind the luggage trolley. Quite a vehicular traffic jam was developing.

'Where do you want these?' the bellboy repeated.

Frances stepped aside and waved her hand vaguely. She was relieved to see him push the trolley forward and turn down a passageway. It appeared that he had his own ideas about where the luggage ought to go and had only sought token permission. Of course, he knew the layout of the hotel suite better than any of them.

Frances turned to the bellboy piloting the other wheelchair and waved her hand again. He moved off immediately. Obviously he, too, had his own idea of the proper place to deposit Mr Moskva.

That left Laurenda, eyes still closed. Frances walked behind that wheelchair and a quiet investigation revealed a small handbrake at the back. She released the handbrake and pushed the chair forward into the sitting-room. Laurenda did not stir.

Twinkle was slouched in an armchair, a snowdrift of discarded newspapers around her feet. She looked up only to complain. 'There are eight newspapers here and I'm not mentioned in *any* of them. What's the matter with these people?'

'You only just got here, baby.' Laurenda opened her eyes with what seemed great effort. 'Wait for the afternoon editions. There were lots of reporters at the airport, remember?'

'*And* that lousy photographer,' Twinkle said. 'I'll bet he took my bad side.'

'Oh, I don't think so, honey. You were careful to keep it turned away from them – '

'There ought to be advance publicity, too.' Twinkle cut off her mother's placating whine. 'What's Herkie been doing over here all this time?' She discarded another section of tabloid.

'He's been working hard, I'm sure.' Laurenda began to show signs of animation. 'It takes time to set up all the production angles – '

'Uh-huh.' Twinkle hurled the last of the unsatisfactory newspapers to the floor. 'You always stick up for him.'

'It isn't fair to criticize poor Herkie all the time,' her mother protested. 'He's been awfully good to us, darling.'

'The money I make for him, he'd better be! I put that stupid Company of his back on its feet!'

Abruptly, Frances recalled a description she had once read of another child star: 'Thirteen going on forty.' It seemed to be endemic to the profession.

The doorbell and the telephone rang simultaneously. Neither Twinkle nor her mother took any notice.

Frances picked up the phone, said, 'Could you hold on for just a moment, please,' and dashed for the door. Twinkle and her mother seemed to accept this as a proper course of events. It was beginning to dawn on Frances that her job might not be exactly as Mr Herkimer had described it.

She swung open the door and stepped back just in time as Cecile Savoy, OBE, grande dame of stage and cinema swept in, followed by a television leading man who was familiar, but not a 'name'. In fact, Frances could not put a name to him, but recognized that he was probably destined for an appropriate part in the film.

'Where is she?' Cecile Savoy, in full cry, headed unerringly for the sitting-room. 'Where is our dear little co-star?'

The young man drifted in her wake somewhat

uncertainly. He appeared less certain of their welcome. Perhaps he had heard rumours about their dear little co-star. He was carrying a long, tissue-wrapped object and he appeared to be having some doubts about that, as well.

Cecile Savoy halted in the doorway, posing there until she was certain all eyes were upon her, then she swept forward into the room, advancing on Twinkle.

'My *dear* child – ' she announced. 'My dear, dear child. How sweet you look.'

'We didn't ring for anything,' Twinkle said flatly. 'What are you doing here?'

Cecile Savoy halted in mid-stride, her smile congealing.

'Twinkle, that isn't very nice,' her mother reproved. 'What she means – ' Laurenda turned to Cecile Savoy – 'is, er – '

'I mean, who are you?' Twinkle could deal with the lower orders herself. 'And what are you doing here?'

The young man, already partially hidden behind Cecile Savoy, retreated a few more steps. He appeared to have a nervous disposition.

'Julian!' Cecile Savoy rounded on him. He hadn't moved fast enough – or far enough. 'Julian, tell this . . . *creature* who I am!'

'Oh yes, of course.' He started nervously and came forward half a step. 'Miss, er, Twinkle, this is Cecile Savoy, your co-star. She's playing Miss Minchin.'

'Yeah?' Twinkle turned disbelieving eyes upon him, but at least kept private her opinion of the status of other players in relation to her own. 'And who are *you*?'

'This is Julian Favely,' Cecile Savoy said. 'One of

our most brilliant and talented rising young stars,' she added, perhaps magnanimously, or perhaps to show him the way she considered an introduction ought to be performed. 'He will be playing the dual role of Ram Dass and Mr Carmichael.'

'We're doing it on the cheap again, are we?' Unimpressed, Twinkle continued to regard them both with a basilisk stare. 'So what are you doing here now? Shooting doesn't start until next week.'

From the flash of Cecile Savoy's eyes, shooting would have started immediately, if only she had had the forethought to have brought along a gun. Hostilities had definitely been declared.

'Say – ' The man who had disappeared into the kitchen reappeared in the other doorway, the young woman behind him. 'We've just been investigating the kitchen and it's all equipped – with food, even. Why don't we – ' He noticed the others and broke off.

'Dick,' Laurenda began, 'this is – '

'You needn't tell me.' He started forward, hand outstretched. 'I would recognize Cecile Savoy anywhere. I've been a fan of hers since – since – ' Again he broke off, took her hand and, bowing low, kissed it. 'It will be an honour to work with you.'

Frances noted with interest that, whoever he was, he had obviously been around actresses long enough to realize the indelicacy of being too specific about years.

'How kind of you,' Cecile Savoy purred. 'And *I* am very pleased to meet *you*?' She made it both a statement and a question.

'Forgive me,' he said immediately, 'I'm Dick Brouder. I'm directing this picture.'

'At the moment,' Twinkle muttered.

'*Please*, baby.' Her mother turned agonized eyes towards her. 'You *promised*.'

'Just don't rock the boat then,' Twinkle said darkly. 'That's all.'

'And this – ' Dick Brouder went on smoothly, ignoring the exchange between Twinkle and her mother. 'This is Ilse Carlsson, our costume designer.' He beckoned forward the girl who had been exploring the suite with him.

'Your sketches were enchanting, my dear,' Cecile Savoy said. 'I understand we have costume fittings in the morning. I shall look forward to trying on all those lovely creations. It's been years since I've been in a costume piece.'

'Huh! She probably wore outfits like those the *first* time round!'

'*Please*, baby, don't – '

'Er – ' Julian Favely stepped forward, holding out his parcel propitiatingly. 'Perhaps we ought to give her the present we brought – ?'

'Yes!' Cecile Savoy whirled on him and snatched the parcel from his hands. 'For *you*, my dear.' She bestowed it on Ilse Carlsson.

'Why, thank you.' Pleased, but faintly puzzled, obviously suspecting unknown nuances, Ilse wrestled with a shroud of tissue paper.

'Oh!' She gasped with delight as a large doll dressed as Queen Elizabeth I, complete with crown and sceptre, emerged from the wrappings. 'Oh, it's exquisite!'

'I knew *you'd* appreciate it,' Cecile Savoy said smugly.

'Thank you! Thank you!' Ilse was investigating the

costume. 'Look!' She held it out to Dick Brouder. 'Every detail is authentic. It's fantastic.'

But Dick Brouder was gazing beyond her with an anxious look. Laurenda, too, was watching Twinkle with the uneasy air of someone expecting a major explosion; aware that it was inevitable, powerless to prevent it.

Twinkle sank lower in her chair, ostentatiously picked up one of the newspapers from the floor, and buried herself in its pages. The room was charged with the brooding atmosphere of an impending storm.

'Ah, this is where everybody is!' Mr Herkimer was abruptly in their midst. Frances hadn't been aware of the doorbell but, of course, Mr Herkimer would have his own key.

'You've all met each other? Everybody is friends.' He asked and answered his own question. 'Now, let's have a little party. I ordered the fridge stocked with goodies and – '

'I fear we have a previous engagement,' Cecile Savoy said. 'We merely stopped by to welcome . . . everyone. Come, Julian.'

She was as brilliant at exits as at entrances. She swept out, followed by Julian Favely who was not nearly so expert at giving the impression of an entire retinue. He looked back over his shoulder, sketched a half-apologetic smile and tripped over the rug, righting himself just in time. The door closed behind them with a firm click that was somehow more disquieting than an outright slam.

'Well,' Mr Herkimer looked uneasily at the others. '*We* will have a little party, eh?'

Belatedly, Frances remembered the telephone and

returned to it, but the caller had obviously given up long ago. She replaced the receiver thoughtfully.

'I'm afraid I don't feel up to a party, Herkie,' Laurenda said. 'I'd just like to go to bed and catch up on my sleep.'

'Ilse and I have tickets for a show,' Dick Brouder said quickly. 'It's the last night –' They began moving quietly towards the door.

'Then *we* – ' Mr Herkimer broke off as Frances avoided his pleading eye. She had been on active duty less than a complete day, but already felt that she needed time to recover.

'I want to sleep, too,' Twinkle declared abruptly, not lowering her paper. 'The rest of you can do what you like – *I* don't care!'

But she *did* care. Frances had caught the expression on her face as Cecile Savoy had given the doll – *her* doll – to Ilse Carlsson. She had seen the subsequent expression as Ilse had lifted the exquisite creation from its tissue paper nest.

Twinkle had wanted that doll, wanted it desperately. The fact that she had lost it through her own rudeness and bad temper had nothing to do with the matter in her self-centred, immature mind. She felt that she had been balked of what was rightfully hers – and someone was going to pay for it.

Perhaps they were all going to pay.

CHAPTER V

At any rate, the hours were convenient, Frances decided the next morning. When she let herself into the suite at 10.00 a.m. with her duplicate key, there was no sign of anyone having stirred yet.

The complete set of morning newspapers, including the *Financial Times*, was on the console table in the foyer, beside a small pile of letters. Someone had stirred then, if only the hotel staff.

There was an eerieness about standing in the silent hallway, surrounded by sleeping strangers. Was this the way a burglar felt as he began his task?

Frances turned and went into the sitting-room, almost on tiptoe, although the thickness of the carpet would have absorbed any amount of normal noise. It would take a heavy body hitting the floor to raise a thud from that carpet.

And *that* was not the sort of thought one needed, alone in strange surroundings.

Really, Frances assured herself, the place could not be safer. It was simply the insulation from the outside world that produced this strange feeling of isolation. But the world was all around them – the sitting-room, restored to impersonality by unseen hands, proved that. Somewhere beyond the silent corridors of the sleeping suite, life went on.

A sharp click elsewhere in the suite startled her. It appeared that life was going on in here, too. She went to investigate.

A further sound, a chinking, as of crockery being displaced, guided her to the kitchen.

The refrigerator door stood open, strange striped bulges protruding all around it. It looked rather as though the appliance had swallowed someone and was having trouble digesting him.

'Mr Moskva?' Frances asked, although there was no one else it could possibly have been.

'Yuh?' A face like a crater-shadowed full moon popped into view over the top of the door, the sound of rattling dishes continued in the depths of the fridge.

'I'm Frances Armitage – she began.

'Oh, yuh. We probably met. Forgive me if I don't remember.' He dived back into the fridge.

'Actually, we didn't meet,' she said. 'You were asleep – '

'I was out cold,' he corrected, in the interest of accuracy. 'It's the only way to fly.'

'You may be right.' Frances watched in fascination as a mound of food began to sprout on top of the refrigerator. Obviously, last night's party had been a complete failure and poor Mr Herkimer had ordered enough supplies to feed several armies. It was a pity that such delicacies never looked quite so good the next day.

'I guess that's all.' Reluctantly, Morris Moskva stepped back from the fridge and closed the door. 'It will have to do.'

'Shall I help you carry it into the dining-room?' Frances asked.

'Naw.' Three cocktail sausages and a lump of cheese disappeared into his mouth. 'If I don't eat something fast, I won't be able to make it to the dining-room.' A handful of miniature vol-au-vents followed the sausages.

'I see.' Frances smiled weakly.

'I'm sorry, I'm forgetting my manners.' He lifted a platter of assorted canapés and thrust it towards her. 'Have something yourself. Please.'

'Well . . .' She realized that her own manners would be lacking if she failed to join him. Worse, such a failure might be misconstrued as criticism. 'Thank you, I will.'

His anxious eyes followed her hovering hand as it passed the small spicy meatballs, the devilled eggs, the rollmop herrings. His sigh of relief was almost audible as she chose a limp cracker spread with cream cheese already showing drought marks after a night in the refrigerator.

'You're sure that's what you want?' His other hand swept over the platter in a sleight-of-hand gesture. All the spicy meatballs disappeared and his cheek bulged suddenly. 'Have something else.'

'No, no, thank you.' Frances stepped back as he thrust the platter forward aggressively. 'I had breakfast before I left home. That's enough.'

'You're right.' He surveyed the platter gloomily and poked amongst the remaining items with a critical thumb and forefinger. Abruptly, the rollmop herrings disappeared. 'I'll phone down to Room Service for a decent breakfast. This stuff wouldn't keep a bird alive.'

'You're sure –' Frances glanced at the suddenly bare platter – 'you can make it as far as the dining-room now?'

'Yuh.' He grinned at her, one hand already groping towards the top of the fridge for another dish of sustenance. 'Just about.' His grin widened. 'Where did they find you? You're going to fit in just great.'

'I answered an advertisement in *The Times*,' Frances told him absently, wondering if she ought to cancel her subscription. 'Mr Herkimer asked me along for an interview and, before I knew it, I was hired.'

'Good old Herkie.' Morris Moskva shook his head admiringly. 'He may not look too bright, but he never puts a foot wrong.'

'Thank you,' Frances said, deducing a compliment somewhere in his words.

'That is, hardly ever,' he qualified his words cautiously. 'Twinkle, I'm not so sure about. Personally, I'd rather be working with a couple of tons of dynamite. At least, with dynamite, you've got some idea what will set it off and you can be careful. But that kid – ' He shook his head again, forebodingly, this time.

'Surely, she's just a harmless child . . .' Frances's automatic protest dwindled away. There had been something in Twinkle's attitude, even in the short time she had had to observe her, that was not particularly childlike.

'Child, maybe,' Morris Moskva summed it up briskly for her. 'Harmless, I'm not so sure. I could tell you some stories – ' He paused, frowning darkly. 'A friend of mine worked on her picture before last. He was a nice guy.'

'*Was*?' Frances prompted, when he seemed inclined to leave it at that.

'No, no, nothing like that. He's coming along fine,' Morris assured her. 'The shrinks say they'll let him out in another couple of months.'

'If she's that bad – ' Frances hesitated.

'I won't say he wasn't heading for a breakdown any-how – she just hurried it along. But what were you going to say?'

'I was going to say, I'm a bit surprised that you're here working with her. I'm rather surprised that any-one is.'

'A job's a job, and she's hot right now. Besides, I've worked with kid stars before.' He shrugged. 'I've seen them come and I've seen them go. Especially, I've seen them go. They don't last long. A few years at the top and then they're nowhere. How many can you think of who've ever made it in the adult league?'

'Why, er –' Thus challenged, Frances found that her mind immediately went blank.

'There are the obvious examples, but you can count them on the fingers of one hand, right? Then there are a few more that we know of in the States, but you don't see them over here because their big new career is doing television commercials and trading on the name they established for themselves twenty, maybe thirty, years ago. So everybody can stare at them and say, "My, how they've grown," and "Look, wrinkles." It's just another kind of circus sideshow, and they're the freaks. Mind you, I'm not saying they weren't probably freaks to begin with. Or, if they weren't, a few years of stardom turned them into freaks.'

Brooding, he absently cleared a dish of olives and peanuts.

'They *must* have a difficult life,' Frances murmured sympathetically.

'Not half as difficult as they make life for everybody around them.' He raised his eyes from the denuded dishes on top of the fridge and inspected Frances, 'So, you're the new nursemaid, huh?'

'I'm not sure what I am,' Frances confessed. 'I've been hired as Twinkle's chaperone and secretary, but no one has given me any information about what exactly that entails.'

'I'm not surprised. If they'd told you, you wouldn't be here now. However, I can help you out with a few basic principles.' He began ticking them off on his fingers.

'One, keep your guard up. Two, protect yourself in the clinches. Three, forget the Marquess of Queensbury Rules – this kid never heard of them and, if she had, she'd use them as a guide on how to behave. Not that she needs much guiding. She goes for the jugular vein by instinct.'

Glaring at his extended finger, he found several grains of salt and paused to lick them off.

'If you believe that,' Frances said slowly, 'I'm even more surprised that you're willing to work with her.'

'There's not much the kid can do to me.' He shrugged. 'A literary critic she's not – and nobody's going to pay any attention to her views on the script. That's all that needs to concern me.'

'Just the same – '

'Besides, she's got plenty more to worry about than me. I rank pretty low in the Knifing Order. But, believe me, there's a couple of people around here whose shoes I wouldn't be in for anything. Why *they* took the job, I don't know – well, maybe I can guess. But there isn't that much money in the world – '

'Who?' Frances could not resist asking.

'Never mind.' He lumbered forward and took her arm. 'I've been talking too much.' He led her towards the dining-room. 'And, besides, it may never happen. The kid's growing up. Maybe some sense will set in.'

'But if – '

'Come on, let's go phone Room Service and get some breakfast before I die of hunger.' He propelled her along.

'Oh!' From the corner of her eye, she caught a flutter of movement as they passed one of the bed-rooms. Which one? And had the occupant been standing just inside the door – or even outside in the corridor? – for the movement had been one of quick withdrawal. If so, how loudly had they been speaking, and how much had been overheard?

'What's the matter?' Intent on reaching the tele-phone to order fresh supplies of food, Morris Moskva had noticed nothing.

'I thought I saw – ' Before she could finish, the door-bell rang.

'Here we go.' He gave her a gentle push towards the door. 'Now the circus starts again. You'd better let them in.'

'But – '

The doorbell rang again, more insistently. Morris Moskva noticed the extension telephone in the foyer and headed for it. Frances gave up the attempt at communication and opened the door. Behind her, somewhere in the suite, she heard a sleepy voice raised in complaint at the noise.

Ilse Carlsson and Dick Brouder rushed into the suite as Frances stepped back from the door. They appeared to be in the midst of a private argument and barely nodded as they made straight for the sitting-room. Ilse snapped open her portfolio in mid-stride and pulled out a handful of sketches and swatches of materials. Frances caught the words 'Costume fittings'.

She closed the door, then had to open it again hurriedly as the bell pealed once more. This time, two nondescript girls, bearing limp dresses over their arms, and a bellboy lurched in under the weight of several bolts of material. They surged across the foyer and headed for the sitting-room, where they could hear Ilse's voice raised in anger.

Frances looked down the outside corridor before closing the door again, and then leaned against it thoughtfully for a moment. It appeared that the working day had now begun.

CHAPTER VI

In no time, the suite was alive with people. Strangers came and went, some making deliveries, some on unexplained missions. There was a script conference in the sitting-room, costume fittings in Twinkle's bedroom, and huddles of anonymous people occupied odd corners engrossed in mysterious problems of their own.

Like herself, Dick Brouder appeared to have become a permanent occupant of the reception area. He raced up and down it endlessly in response to frequent urgent wails for his attention, which was necessary to settle some point or other.

'You're sticking *pins* in me!' Twinkle's shrill whine rose in competition with the doorbell.

Frances hurried to answer the bell. At one point, she

had tried to ignore it, but so had everyone else and the insistent ringing had worn her down. She wasn't sure whether or not it was part of her job but, as no one else appeared willing to take it on, she seemed to have won it by default.

'I'm here for the costume fitting.' Cecile Savoy swept past her, a black Pekinese tucked under one arm.

'In there.' Frances indicated the bedroom, from which there floated an indignant, '*Ouch!* That *hurt!*'

Cecile Savoy flinched at the sound of Twinkle's voice, but was the stuff of which the grand old troupers were made. Gripping her Pekinese more firmly, she advanced on the room.

Just as Dick Brouder dashed out of it. He managed to turn the threatened collision into a swift, side-stepping embrace and dashed past her in answer to a voice raised in urgent summons from the script conference.

'. . . want to talk to Frances for a minute. I'll be right back, baby.'

Hearing her name, Frances turned. Laurenda came slowly out of the bedroom and gave her a wan smile. 'It's getting awfully hot in there,' she said in explanation. ' And Twinkle *fusses* so. She hates fittings.'

'Children usually do,' Frances murmured, watching her.

'I suppose so.' Laurenda crossed the foyer, slowly and wearily, as though she were decades older than the years that showed on her face. Fleetingly, Frances wondered just what illness she had. No one had ever specified. 'But she seems to fuss more than most kids. She always did.' Laurenda sighed 'I guess it's only natural, though.'

'Very natural,' Frances agreed. 'The pressures of stardom, and all that.'

'Exactly.' Laurenda brightened faintly and looked around her. 'People don't always understand that. They forget Twinkle is carrying the whole picture. Without her, where would any of them be?'

'The pressures are enormous.' Frances was beginning to feel puzzled. It was quite clear that Laurenda had nothing special to say to her, and she was starting to suspect that Laurenda had no interest in a breath of air, either. Laurenda's eyes kept moving slowly, cautiously, almost slyly, seeking something beyond their range.

'Enormous,' Laurenda echoed. 'On all of us.' She sank down into one of the empty wheelchairs which had been placed beside the foyer table waiting for someone to come and collect them. It was, perhaps, not quite what she had been looking for, but it seemed to be an acceptable substitute at this moment.

'Are you feeling all right?' Frances asked anxiously. 'Shall I get you a glass of water?'

'I'll be all right,' Laurenda said faintly. 'It's just . . .' Her voice trailed off and her eyes closed.

Frances stared down at the woman, wondering if she had fainted. Was she, in truth, seriously ill? Or had Twinkle spent the night throwing tantrums and depriving her mother of much-needed sleep?

There was a final shout from the script conference, and Dick Brouder careered into the corridor again. He stopped short as he saw them and came forward more slowly than Frances had yet seen him move.

'How are you, Laurenda?' he asked. 'Was . . . was everything all right after we left last night?'

'Mostly, it was.' Laurenda opened her eyes. 'But you know what she's like when she gets upset. It took a long while to quieten her down, and then I had to stay with her until she fell asleep.'

'She takes too much out of you.' Dick Brouder frowned down at her. 'More than you can afford. I wish – '

'Maybe I *will* have a glass of water.' Laurenda turned to Frances.

Frances moved away quickly, determined to linger in the kitchen long enough to prove that she could take a hint. So her surmise had been correct and there *had* been tantrums last night. Tantrums which had taken more out of Laurenda than they had taken out of Twinkle.

However, one can spend just so long getting a glass of water. Holding the glass well out before her to signal her approach on a legitimate errand, Frances went back into the foyer.

Dick Brouder was still talking earnestly to Laurenda. Frances paused to gaze abstractedly at a rather frightful hunting print on the wall. Presumably the hotel management did not wish to hang anything good enough to tempt their guests into packing it along with the ashtrays and towels.

She was still waiting hopefully for some signal from Laurenda to advance when a movement just beyond the bedroom door caught her eye. She turned and saw Twinkle standing there, in a ruffled pastel pink costume of unlikely demureness, glaring at her mother and Dick Brouder with a baleful intensity.

Frances moved forward uneasily, no longer worried about permission. It was obvious that they had no idea that they were being observed.

But Twinkle obviously realized that she had been caught spying. Briefly, she transferred her murderous glare to Frances before stepping out of the doorway and confronting her mother.

'I thought you wanted to talk to Frances!' she accused.

'I did, baby. I did talk to her.' Laurenda twitched around to face her child. 'But then Dick just wanted to – to ask me something. About your costumes. And Frances went to get me a drink of water – Here she is now –' Laurenda turned to Frances eagerly, reaching out for the glass of water to prove her story.

'Yeah?' Twinkle looked from one to the other suspiciously. 'Well, watch it! That's all. Just watch it!' She turned and flounced back into the bedroom.

'Thank you, Frances.' Laurenda drained the glass and handed it back. She looked worse than ever.

There was a sudden shriek, a shrill yapping and a shout of defiance from Twinkle. 'I did *not* kick her. I only stepped on her. I didn't see she was there. Why don't you get a dog people can *see*?'

'My poor, poor darling!' Cecile Savoy's voice, trained to reach the top balconies of musical comedy theatres in the days before microphones were standard equipment, swamped Twinkle's feeble bleat easily. 'Poor, sweet Fleur. Did the nasty brat trample all over her with those great big feet?'

'They are not big! And I'll kick her if I want to!'

There were further shrieks, yips and scuffles. Cecile Savoy erupted from the bedroom, holding aloft the black Pekinese. Twinkle was immediately behind her, clutching at a long Victorian skirt which was already coming adrift in a shower of pins, and snatching for the dog.

Following them, Ilse Carlsson clutched alternately at the falling skirt and at Twinkle. 'Please, Miss Savoy. Please, Twinkle,' she wailed distractedly. 'The costumes. You will ruin the lovely costumes.'

'It's a stinking, rotten costume – and I hate it, anyway!' Twinkle tore at her ruffles; they parted from the bodice with a sharp ripping sound. 'There!' Twinkle hurled them at Ilse. 'I hate those awful things. They make me look stupid!'

'Now, Twinkle.' Unwisely, Dick Brouder decided to take a hand. 'They're period costumes, and they're beautiful. You can't play a little Victorian girl wearing jeans. They didn't wear them then.'

'You shut up!' Twinkle whirled on him, momentarily abandoning her attempt to snatch the Pekinese from Cecile Savoy. 'You don't know anything about it. You don't have to wear this junk!'

'It's very nice junk, baby,' Laurenda placated. 'I mean,' she added hastily, with a sideways glance at Ilse Carlsson, who was clutching the detached ruffle with inarticulate fury; 'I mean, it's a beautiful costume. They're all beautiful costumes. You ought to be happy to wear them, honey.'

'Well, I'm not! I hate them!' Twinkle tore at the remainder of the costume. 'And I *won't* wear them, so there!' Several more tatters of costume flew towards Ilse.

Frances regretted that Laurenda had drunk all the water. A quick splash in the face might do Twinkle more good than all the reasoned arguments the others were trying to muster.

'Ill-bred *and* badly brought up.' Cecile Savoy pronounced verdict. 'I suppose we can only be thankful that she's able to read her script.' She paused delicately and, with the timing that had brought a generation of theatregoers to their feet applauding, added, 'She *can* read, I presume?'

'I can read, you old bat! I can read better than you can!'

'I doubt that.' Cecile Savoy lowered the trembling Peke and began stroking it. It was a mistake. Twinkle snatched for the dog again. It began to yelp hysterically.

'Leave Fleur-de-lis alone!' Cecile Savoy snapped.

'Floor — what?' Twinkle drew back her hand. 'Floor mop,' she decided. 'That's what the mutt is. A floor mop!' She snatched for it once more. 'Floor mop! You're an old floor mop!'

'Please, Miss Savoy. Please, Twinkle,' Ilse pleaded. 'The fittings. There is so much to do. Please let us go back and go on with our work.'

'No — I'm bored,' Twinkle protested. 'Fittings are the boringest things in the world. I don't want to do any more today.'

'Please, baby — ' Laurenda drifted slowly out of her wheelchair, as though struggling upwards from full fathom five. 'Be a good girl. Everybody gets bored sometimes. You have to put up with these things to be a star.'

Cecile Savoy snorted. 'It takes more than costumes,' she said.

'You shut up!' Twinkle whirled on her. 'You-just-shut-up!'

'*I* shall finish my costume fitting, like a professional. Here — ' Unexpectedly, the black Pekinese was thrust into Frances's arms. 'Take Fleur downstairs for walkies, would you, my dear? She won't be so restless then.'

Frances clutched at the Peke as it began to slip and backed away from Twinkle, who looked as though she might be going to lunge for the animal again.

'Frances is *my* chaperone – ' Twinkle changed her line of attack. '*You* can't give her orders!'

'Please, baby,' Laurenda said faintly. 'I've got *such* a headache.'

'I gave no orders.' Cecile Savoy drew herself up. 'I simply made a request.'

'But she's *my* chaperone.'

'You are not in need of a chaperone at the moment.' Cecile Savoy looked down on Twinkle. 'I doubt that you ever will be.'

'I hate you!' Twinkle launched herself into a full attack, clawing for Cecile Savoy's face which, fortunately, was well out of reach. 'I *hate* you!'

Cecile Savoy stepped back sharply and Twinkle stumbled, her clawing hands closed on the folds of Cecile's costume as she fought for balance.

In a shower of pins, the waist of the skirt parted from the bodice and the skirt drifted away. Twinkle righted herself and retreated, momentarily aghast.

'Really!' Cecile Savoy turned gracefully, kicking aside the dangling skirt as though it were a court train; the final pins parted and it sank to the floor. Back straight, head erect as though balancing a tiara; Cecile Savoy swept through the doorway, Lady Bracknell in peach crêpe-de-chine Directoire knickers.

'My costume!' Ilse gathered up the folds of material and hurried into the room after her.

Twinkle moved to follow them, but Laurenda held her back. 'Maybe you'd better give them a few minutes, honey,' she said. 'Come out in the kitchen and have a glass of milk, or something.'

'I'm not afraid of *them*,' Twinkle boasted, but she went with her mother just the same.

Frances glanced downwards to meet a world-weary pair of dark brown eyes. Fleur-de-lis, it appeared, was well accustomed to all the varieties of artistic temperament and had only one main concern: would it affect her promised walk?

'All right,' Frances said. 'I suppose we ought to take you downstairs.'

A small grateful yap answered her.

Farther down the hallway, Morris Moskva hovered in the sitting-room doorway, drawn there by the noise of the fracas outside the master bedroom. As Frances passed him, he raised his eyebrows and semaphored *I told you so* to her.

Turning back into the script conference, his voice rose in false cheerfulness. 'It's okay,' he announced. 'There's nothing to worry about. They're *supposed* to hate each other. The script calls for it.'

Perhaps, if he had not talked so frankly to her earlier, Frances would not have noticed the peculiar note in his voice as he added, 'There's no problem. We're off to a flying start.'

CHAPTER VII

Just as Fleur-de-lis was investigating her first lamp post, Mr Herkimer and Julian Favely came along. They halted and Julian surveyed the scene with growing cheer.

'I see I'm just in time,' he said. 'I missed it. So Aunt Cecile roped you in for the necessary, eh?'

Fleur-de-lis squatted and the answer became obvious. Frances looked away and wished that she had something respectable, like a pet rock, at the other end of the leash.

'How are things going?' Mr Herkimer rescued her. 'Everything all right, is it?' he asked in a gloomy tone which betrayed that he knew the answer only too well.

'I'm afraid Twinkle and Miss Savoy have crossed swords again,' Frances said. 'I was glad to get away for a while. The atmosphere was becoming rather fraught.'

'Show me somebody that kid *doesn't* fight with,' Mr Herkimer shrugged.

'You mustn't be too hard on her,' Julian protested. 'Cecile has a neat little armoury of temperamental fireworks when the occasion demands it.'

'Listen.' Mr Herkimer regarded him with a brooding eye. 'At your aunt's age, I figure she's earned the right to sound off a little when she feels like it. But Twinkle –' He shook his head. 'All she's got is, she photographs like a dream – right here and now. Okay, so she can act a little, too. But what's going to happen to her in the future, huh? She's got nothing behind her except a few movies. No stage plays, no repertory, she's never even done anything on television. She came up fast – but she can go down even faster.'

'Perhaps realizing that is what makes her so difficult.' Frances remembered an abrupt movement in a shadowed doorway immediately after Morris Moskva had voiced much the same opinion. It would take a duller child than Twinkle to be unaware of how perilously the crown of stardom perched on her small head – and of how many people would like to see it slip off and tumble into the gutter.

'Anything that happens to that kid in her future – and I hope it's the worst – she's got it coming.' Mr Herkimer glanced upwards at the suite. Frances had the odd, fleeting impression that he was delaying the moment when he would have to enter the hotel.

Fleur-de-lis finished her errand and scampered over to join them, yelping a welcome to Julian. He bent and patted her absently.

'Nevertheless,' he said, 'everyone does seem to be rather hard on the child.'

'Wait until you've been working with her a while. I'll guarantee you volunteer to lead the lynch mob. Anyway – ' Mr Herkimer looked at him suspiciously – 'your own aunt can't stand her, so why are *you* defending her? Whose side are you on?'

'It's not a question of sides,' Julian said. 'Justice, perhaps, but not sides. In any case, Cecile isn't in a mood to stand much of anything these days. Perhaps you've heard?'

'Heard?' Mr Herkimer was instantly alert. 'Heard what? She's not sick, is she? I mean, not fatally? She isn't – ' His voice fell to an anguished croak. 'She isn't going to die before she's finished her scenes in the picture?'

'No, no, nothing like that.' Julian's quick reply did nothing to reassure Mr Herkimer, who continued to gaze at him anxiously. 'You mean, you really haven't heard?' For a moment he looked as suspicious as Mr Herkimer.

'I've heard nothing,' Mr Herkimer said firmly. 'Believe me, if I'd had any doubts, I'd never have signed the contract with Savoy. I've had trouble enough in the past – I mean, my nerves aren't what they used to be and all this kind of worry isn't good for me.'

'It's all right,' Julian assured him. 'I believe you. It's just that Cecile has such a fixation about the whole thing that she's infected me. She thinks everyone knows and is talking about it. She believes the whole London theatrical set is laughing at her.'

'Why? Why?' Mr Herkimer sounded momentarily like Fleur-de-lis in one of her more excitable moments. 'Why should they laugh at her?'

'Because, you see,' Julian looked embarrassed. 'The Honours List came out for the Queen's Birthday – and she wasn't on it . . . again.'

'Honours List?' Mr Herkimer stared at him blankly.

'She expected to be made a Dame. Nearly everyone else in her generation is. Either a Dame or a Knight. Oh, I know she has an OBE, but that isn't the same thing at all. I mean it isn't a title, is it?'

'Isn't it?' It was clear that the intricacies of the English Honours system were lost on Mr Herkimer. He remained baffled.

'Actually, it isn't.' Julian rescued him. 'Aunt Cecile was very disappointed and, the thing is, everyone knew it. That's why she suspects they're laughing at her. The whole episode has put her into a very bad humour, I'm afraid. She's ready to take offence at anything.'

'With Twinkle around, there'll be plenty to take offence at,' Mr Herkimer predicted gloomily.

'But can't her mother control – ?' Frances broke off as they both stared at her.

'Laurenda – control?' Mr Herkimer was incredulous. 'Look, Laurenda tries sometimes – when she's feeling extra strong. But that isn't often. And she's no match for that kid. Besides – ' he shook his head – 'Laurenda's got troubles of her own.'

He turned towards Julian with sudden anxiety, as though silently pleading with him to change to a less painful subject. Julian, puzzled, but receiving the message, tried to oblige.

'Well, come along, old girl.' He stooped and gathered a co-operative Fleur-de-lis into his arms. 'We ought to be getting back upstairs.'

'That's right,' Mr Herkimer seconded eagerly. 'Your aunt will be wondering where you are.'

'Oh!' Julian straightened abruptly. 'Er . . . this is rather awkward. I . . . I must make an earnest request of you . . .' Avoiding all eyes, he stared steadfastly into mid-distance. Small beads of perspiration began to form along his otherwise immaculate hairline

'What's the matter?' Mr Herkimer tried, but failed, to meet his eyes, and settled for a brief agonized exchange of glances with Frances. 'What is it now?'

'About my aunt,' Julian Favely said. 'Aunt Cecile,'

he added, just in case there should be any doubt. 'Please don't tell her. You'll get me into the most frightful trouble.'

'Trouble?' Mr Herkimer still could not capture those evasive eyes. 'What trouble? Tell her what?'

'Well . . . *you* know . . .' Julian Favely clutched Fleur-de-lis so tightly that she whimpered. 'I didn't mean to tell you . . . it slipped out. And then I thought perhaps you wouldn't notice it, but you did. You picked it right up and . . . and she'll be furious. She'll *kill* me if she thinks people know the truth.'

'Know what?' Mr Herkimer was close to shouting. 'What truth? What? What?'

'That she *is* my aunt,' Julian Favely confessed desperately. 'That I'm really her nephew. That we aren't . . . aren't "just good friends" . . .'

'*Good friends!*' Mr Herkimer fell back a step or two. 'You mean that nice, *distinguished*, old lady wants everybody to think – ?'

'Actually, she'd prefer it if they did,' Julian defended stubbornly. 'You can understand it, can't you?'

'Yes,' Frances said.

'No,' Mr Herkimer said.

'You see . . .' Still adamantly refusing to look at them, Julian struggled to explain. 'If she can't be a Dame . . .'

'She'll settle for everybody thinking she's a Dirty Old Lady?' Mr Herkimer asked incredulously.

'It's a matter of saving face,' Julian murmured.

'*Face!*' Mr Herkimer muttered weakly.

'After all,' Frances intervened, 'it would provide a sort of an explanation, wouldn't it?'

'Exactly – ' Julian turned towards her earnestly, almost meeting her eyes in his eagerness. 'If she can convince the Public that the only thing keeping her from a DBE is her private life – '

'I think I've got a headache,' Mr Herkimer announced. 'I always think I've got a little bit of a headache somewhere waiting to close in on me – but now it's pounced.'

'In that case – ' Julian turned away. 'I won't detain you any longer. I'll bring Fleur up to Aun – I mean, up to Cecile . . . And you *will* keep our little secret, won't you?'

'Of course, we will,' Frances assured him.

'Sure. Sure,' Mr Herkimer said. 'Why not? What's one more private problem along with the ones we've already got?'

'It will keep Cecile Savoy happy,' Julian tossed back over his shoulder as he moved towards the hotel.

'Oh, great!' Mr Herkimer moaned. 'That's all we need. We want to keep Cecile Savoy happy. We want to keep Twinkle happy. We want likewise to keep the director, the designer, the scriptwriter, the grips, the electricians and all the Unions happy. Maybe even, someday, *I'll* get the chance to be happy.' He shook his head mournfully.

Julian Favely had disappeared into the hotel, moving with a rapidity which betrayed his anxiety to get away from the scene of his indiscretion. Frances smiled weakly, beginning to wish that she had accompanied him.

'I don't understand women,' Mr Herkimer confessed. 'Especially, I don't understand actresses! Of course,' he brightened, 'women don't understand me, either.'

'Perhaps we ought to join the others,' Frances murmured.

'I've had eight wives – ' Mr Herkimer impaled her with his mournful gaze. 'Not counting the ones I married twice. Just like Henry the Eighth. And not one of them ever really understood me.'

'Henry the Eighth only had six wives.' Frances chose the only portion of the confidence she felt she could answer.

'You mean I beat him?' Mr Herkimer seemed cheered by the thought.

'I really think I ought to get back to Twinkle,' Frances said, more firmly.

'You don't have to worry about that kid,' Mr Herkimer said. 'I'd back her against a den of lions. Which reminds me of what I was saying about my ex-wives – '

'Really, Mr Herkimer,' Frances said. 'I ought to – '

'Herkie, please.' Mr Herkimer was pained. 'I thought we agreed you were going to call me Herkie. Everybody always calls me Herkie. Except for a couple of my wives, who called me – ' He broke off, his memories seemed to have become even more painful. 'But I guess we don't have to go into that.'

'I'm sure we don't.' Frances began edging towards the sanctuary of the hotel lobby. 'But we really must go back – '

'Back to the *actresses*!' Mr Herkimer sighed heavily, accepting the decision. He allowed her to precede him into the revolving door, then crowded into the same section with her, pushing the door around with what seemed to be a barely-controlled fury.

Perhaps, Frances thought, it reminded him of his marital life.

'If you dislike actresses so,' Frances asked reasonably, 'why did you go into the cinema?'

'I didn't know any better.' Brooding, Mr Herkimer shot them out into the lobby and, taking Frances by the arm, aimed her at the bank of lifts.

'That was what my mother said to me. "Herkie," she said, "don't do this terrible thing. Go into the rag trade like your Uncle Hymie, your Uncle Myron, your Cousin Sid." I shoulda listened to her. But did I listen? Naw!'

He jabbed at the top button and doors slid closed silently behind them and the lift zoomed upwards.

'Naw, I was too wisenheimer. I knew what I wanted. The movies – that was where it was all happening. So I went into them and I found out. Glamour – hah!'

'It hasn't been *that* unfortunate, has it?' Frances tried to soothe him before they arrived – there was already enough temperament seething through Twinkle's suite. 'I mean, you've been very successful. Everyone knows your name. Your productions always make a profit at the box office – '

'They do now, but there was a time in the Sixties – I don't want to think about the Sixties. Let's forget them – but they've left their mark.' Mr Herkimer turned a haggard countenance to her. 'Look at the price I pay. My private life is shot to hell. An ulcer I've got, maybe two. And always, always, I'm surrounded by madmen. And actresses!' He relapsed into brooding.

'Here we are.' Frances moved forward with relief as the lift halted and the doors slid open.

'Here we are . . .' Mr Herkimer echoed on a dying note. His footsteps lagged as he followed her down the corridor.

'Wait a minute – ' He caught her hand as she started to press the doorbell and looked into her eyes earnestly.

'It isn't always going to be like this, you know,' he assured her.

'Like what?' He had only succeeded in making her more nervous.

'All this hysteria – ' He gestured widely with his other hand. 'It will be better – more disciplined – once we get on the floor. You take the weekend off – you've earned it. And Monday, we start shooting. It will be better then.'

'It will?' Frances wondered whether she ought to remind him that he was still holding her hand. 'With all those other children around? Won't that make Twinkle more . . . er . . . temperamental than ever?'

'What other kids?' For an instant he was puzzled, then his face cleared. 'Oh, you're going by the original book? Don't worry. There won't be any other kids around. Twinkle sees to that. It's even in her contract. She's the only kid on the set.'

'But – '

'Anyhow, we've already shot the scenes with the other kids. While they were on school holidays. By the time we've intercut the close-ups we'll be shooting of Twinkle, and do some re-dubbing, you'll never guess she wasn't surrounded by the other brats in all those scenes. She wants it that way – and it's not only easier, it works out cheaper.'

'Then there aren't going to be dozens of new people to encounter next week?' Frances felt partly relieved, partly cheated at this realization.

'Nope. The Unit's as big as it's going to get – except for the technicians, of course. But you won't have them underfoot. They know their jobs and they'll get on with them. Like I told you, your job is to chaperone Twinkle

– not that she needs it, but the English law says she's got to have a chaperone.'

'Well,' Frances said dubiously, 'I'll do my best.' In the ensuing silent struggle to regain the use of her hand – she was beginning to think she might need a chaperone herself – she managed to stab the doorbell home.

'If you have any problems' – Mr Herkimer squeezed her hand – 'any problems at all, you come straight to Herkie with them, okay? You promise?'

'Okay,' Frances said, distraught. 'I mean, yes. I . . . I promise.'

The door swung open and Twinkle stood there, surveying them both. 'Oh!' Her jaundiced gaze locked on Frances's imprisoned hand. 'He's at it again, is he?'

'I'll kill that kid!' Mr Herkimer muttered, dropping Frances's hand abruptly as they moved forward into the suite. 'So help me, someday I'm going to do the world a favour and murder that brat!'

CHAPTER VIII

'Drink your milk, Twinkle,' Laurenda whined. 'Please drink your nice milk, baby.'

'If it's so nice,' Twinkle said, '*you* drink it.'

'Now, don't be like that, honey. You know it's good for you. You've got to drink it.'

'I won't!'

The battle had been raging intermittently throughout the first week of filming and seemed more virulent than usual this morning. The unwilling spectators were, if possible, even more bored than Twinkle with the subject.

Fortunately, the skirmishes only occurred in the breaks between actual filming and, thanks to Mr Herkimer's careful planning, filming had been proceeding steadily. While the cameras were on her, Twinkle was good as gold. It was when the cameras ceased to turn that the dross showed through.

Cecile Savoy had long ago raised eyes heavenwards and retreated behind the *Telegraph* between shots.

They were ready for shooting again now and the Continuity Girl, who had already developed a harassed look, came forward to compare her check list against Twinkle's actual appearance.

'You had your hat tilted to the left, with a curl escaping from it.' She reached out and made the necessary adjustments.

'I don't like it that way! It looks stupid.' Twinkle tore the hat off, swept her hair off her forehead and rammed the hat back on foursquare.

'Please, Twinkle,' Dick Brouder said patiently. 'If you change everything, we won't be able to match the shots with the shots we've already taken. You know that.'

'They're silly shots, anyway.' Twinkle fidgeted as her mother and the Continuity Girl readjusted her costume. 'And I *wasn't* wearing my hat that way. It was the way I just had it. If you change it, *you'll* be wrong.'

'You don't remember, baby,' Laurenda soothed. 'Nobody can ever remember all those tiny details. That's why Continuity notes everything down. It's her job – she *has* to be right.'

'Well, she isn't!' Twinkle gave Continuity a poisonous

look. 'You'll find out when they develop the shots and then we'll have to do everything all over again and I'm bored with it right now. So why don't we – ?'

'Places, please,' Dick Brouder ordered, cutting across her protest.

Twinkle glared at him, but moved out under the lights. Cecile Savoy rose from her chair, folding her newspaper meticulously. Fleur-de-lis took the opportunity to leap up on the vacated chair with a gleeful yap.

'I don't see why we have to have *animals* all over the place,' Twinkle complained.

Cecile Savoy looked over Twinkle's head vaguely. 'So many obituaries,' she said, dropping the paper to the floor. 'And always for the wrong people.'

'Places!' Dick Brouder snapped, before the combatants had a chance to clash again.

Frances glanced at her watch, waiting to begin the timing when Dick gave the signal for the cameras to start. As her job had been explained to her – rather sketchily, it must be admitted – children were permitted to work only in short stretches, totalling not more than three-and-a-half hours in an eight-hour day. Usually, this meant fifteen minutes of rehearsal and fifteen minutes of filming at a time, but Twinkle had already rehearsed this scene.

'Hold it!' Dick Brouder shouted, just as everyone was expecting the signal. They all looked at him.

'All right, Twinkle,' he said. 'You know we can't have that.'

'I'm not doing anything,' Twinkle protested.

'Twinkle!'

'I'm not!' She backed away as he advanced. '*What*

am I doing? What?'

'The gum, Twinkle.' His face was stern. 'Get rid of it.'

'Nobody can see it. I'm not chewing. Nobody will even know it's there.'

'Get rid of it, Twinkle!'

'Oh, all right.' With deliberately maddening slowness, Twinkle sauntered over to the sidelines and carefully parked her wad of gum beneath the arm of a chair. Someone, somewhere, meshed gears with an effect of grinding teeth.

'That filthy habit!' Cecile Savoy shuddered. 'How I hated it when I was playing in New York. They won't throw their gum away, they always want to retrieve it later – if it hasn't spread all over someone else's clothing in the meantime. *Must* we put up with that on this set?'

'I'll get rid of it,' Laurenda placated hastily. She scrabbled for the gum – it came away in strands clinging to her fingers.

'Here – use this.' Mr Herkimer had arrived on the set in time to assess the situation. He tore a half page from the *Telegraph* and handed it to Laurenda.

'I hadn't finished reading that,' Cecile Savoy announced icily.

'I'll get you another one.' He snapped his fingers and someone detached from the fringe of a group and dashed off.

'And you – ' He turned to Twinkle. 'You cut it out. From now on, if you've gotta chew gum, get rid of it when the shooting starts. Don't just park it – get rid of it! Okay?'

Twinkle gave him a mutinous glare, then ostentatiously turned her back on him and stalked away.

'She'll do it,' Mr Herkimer said, with more confidence than he appeared to feel as his anxious gaze followed Twinkle.

'I don't feel so good,' Laurenda said faintly. 'I think I'd better go lie down for a while.'

'Sure, Laurenda, sure,' Mr Herkimer said. 'That's why we've got a couch in Twinkle's dressing-room. You go and rest.'

'You can handle things here, can't you, Frances?' Laurenda paused for reassurance.

'Oh yes,' Frances said, hoping she sounded more confident than she felt. (Twinkle seemed to inspire mass insecurity.) 'It all seems perfectly straightforward.'

Perfectly straightforward. Presumably it was – once one knew what one was supposed to be doing. It also helped to have discovered what everyone else was supposed to be doing.

Upon arrival at the studio at the beginning of the week, Frances had been taken in tow by a well-meaning, but rather abstracted, Morris Moskva.

She had learned that the Technical Crew were called by the names of the jobs they did, rather along the lines of Welsh usage. Thus, Sparks was the electrician, Props was the property master, Camera the cameraman, Chips the carpenter, and so on.

The most vital member of the Unit, however, was the First Assistant Director, known as 'First', whose job it was, Morris explained, 'to put a big glass bubble around the Director' and protect him from all outside annoyances and distractions, so that he could concentrate on the actors and the film.

'Only,' Morris had added, 'on this picture, it's the actors Dick needs protection from. Especially Twinkle.' However, Frances was left in no doubt that, in case of problems, she was to 'Tell it to First'.

After Morris Moskva had departed in response to a request for consultation on a point in the next scene to be filmed, Frances went in search of First. She felt the need for more of a job definition than Mr Herkimer had given her. She only hoped that First could provide it.

'The chaperone's job?' First's bright blue eyes opened wide and a ripple of surprise wrinkled his fair pink skin, leaving it smooth and expressionless as soon as it had passed.

'Dead easy. Piece of cake.' He beamed down at her. 'No experience necessary. And it's holiday-time, so you won't be clashing with the teacher we'd have to employ if it were term-time. You're quite lucky. A chaperone can be responsible for as many as five children – but you only have to worry about Twinkle.'

'She's enough,' Frances said dryly.

'The rules are simple,' he went on. 'But a bit archaic. It's even law that a child has to be given a hot drink as soon as it arrives on set in the morning. The little darlings don't half create when they're given a cup of hot chocolate in the middle of a heat wave! Fortunately, the law doesn't say we have to force it down their throats. But, you see what I mean? Archaic. Remnants of the days when they sent the little ones down the mines, or up chimneys – as though *we'd* kill any geese laying golden eggs!

'However, basically, a child can't start work before 9.30 a.m. and can't continue working after 4.30 p.m. –

under the age of ten. They can't work more than three-and-a-half hours in any one eight-hour day. They have to have plenty of breaks for rest – luckily, these occur automatically when we're setting up different scenes. They usually work two hours in the morning and an hour-and-a-half in the afternoon. The child can only work 32 days during the year – dubbing time and radio appearances not included. But that doesn't signify with Twinkle – although she comes under English law, she isn't going to be in the country that long. We've been shooting around her for weeks, so that we could bunch her scenes when she arrived and finish the picture in short order.'

'So I stay with Twinkle at all times and – '

'And you just watch that we don't overwork her,' First said. 'Not that we'd have the chance. That kid knows more about her rights than any of us. The most important part of your job is to keep a record of the hours she works and the breaks she takes every day. That's so the Inspector can see that everything's aboveboard when he drops in.'

'What Inspector? When does he drop in?' There were more ramifications to this job than she had suspected.

'The Inspector from the Borough Authority. We never know when he's coming, but he has to visit the set at least once to make sure the regulations are being observed and that all the children are happy. Actually, he came last month when we were doing the school scenes with a lot of kids. He may come again just to have a look at Twinkle, or he may not – we're not sure. But it keeps everyone on their toes.

'You see, if he finds anything he doesn't approve of, he has the power to shut down the whole Unit. Just

like that!' First made a downward sweeping movement
with his hand, looking grimly appalled at the thought
he had just uttered. Or perhaps it was that he had just
been struck by a newer, more appalling thought.

'No,' he said. 'That's silly, isn't it?' He looked to
Frances for reassurance.

'What is?' Frances asked.

'I know she's a little hellion,' he said apologetically.
'That's common knowledge. But she wouldn't pull a
trick *that* dirty, would she?'

Frances shook her head mutely, not following his
train of thought.

'You're right, of course, she wouldn't.' He seemed
only slightly relieved. 'But you *will* keep very good
records, won't you? Make sure you put down every
break and rest period. Then, if she should decide to lie
to the Inspector, we can count on you to prove it isn't
true.'

'She wouldn't do that.' Frances was not quite so
shocked at the idea as she might have been a few weeks
ago – before she had met Twinkle. 'Why should she?'

'Probably not. But, just in case . . .' First met her eyes
nervously. 'You see, if anything goes wrong with the
production, if the Unit shuts down . . . it means she
can go back to the States, doesn't it? It won't make any
difference to *her*, her money is guaranteed. But the rest
of us will be out of jobs. And, you may have heard, the
film industry isn't exactly coining it these days.'

'I'll certainly keep accurate records,' Frances said.
'But,' she added firmly, 'I'm sure Twinkle wouldn't do
anything like that. You're misjudging her.'

'Perhaps I am,' First shrugged. 'As they say, "Give a
dog a bad name" . . .' He brightened. 'In any case, the

Inspector may not come back. She may never get the chance.'

'Cut!' Dick Brouder yelled.

The arc lights went out, the scene they had illumi-nated dissolved into darkness. Cecile Savoy whisked a handkerchief out of her sleeve and dabbed at her face, careful not to disturb her make-up.

Twinkle's face lost its angelic expression and resumed its normal truculence. She turned away and walked off the set; fishing in her muff, she brought out a packet of gum, unwrapped two sticks and jammed them into her mouth, letting the wrappers flutter to the floor. An anonymous figure darted forward and cleared them away.

'Where's Laurenda?' Twinkle demanded peremp-torily as she came up to Frances.

'Your mother is lying down in your dressing-room,' Frances said. 'She doesn't feel well.'

'Again?' Twinkle sighed heavily, then noticed Frances glancing at her watch and entering a figure on the Report form attached to the clipboard which had been issued to her when she arrived on the set. 'What are you doing that for? Nobody ever bothers about those things.'

'*I* intend to bother about them,' Frances said warningly. If Twinkle knew that from the beginning, it might cut off any half-formed ideas she might have.

'Suit yourself,' Twinkle shrugged. 'But people will only think you're being silly.' She chewed thoughtfully for a moment, then unwrapped yet another stick of gum and folded it into her mouth.

The untasted glass of milk stood on the table between

them. Twinkle ignored it and Frances did not think it worth risking her precarious authority by mentioning it. Let Laurenda fight that battle. Twinkle looked healthy enough to be able to skip a few glasses of milk without any dire consequences.

Frances averted her eyes from the milk, and Twinkle smiled faintly. An undeclared truce stretched between them.

'Frances – Frances – ' Mr Herkimer swooped upon them with a tall silent man at his heels. 'I want you should meet my friend and partner. He's just back from California and he'll be with us for the rest of the picture here. Tor Torrington – the other half of Herkimer-Torrington Productions.'

'The better half,' Twinkle muttered.

'Ah, sweet child.' Mr Herkimer patted Twinkle on the head. 'Isn't it wonderful, the way she articulates so well with all that gum in her mouth?'

'I could do it in front of the cameras, too.' Twinkle gave him a poisonous glare and he snatched back his hand hastily. 'If you'd let me.'

'That's out of the question and we will not discuss it again.' Tor Torrington, it seemed, was a different kettle of fish. There would be no nervous currying of favour by him, no matter how bright the star.

'How do you do, Mrs Armitage.' Leaving Twinkle thoroughly quelled, he shook hands solemnly with Frances. 'I'm very glad you could join the Unit at such short notice. Herkie speaks highly of you.'

'Thank you,' Frances said. 'But I'm afraid Mr Her – Herkie speaks highly of everyone.'

'Not everyone,' Mr Herkimer muttered. He bent down and patted Fleur-de-lis, who had trotted over

with her mistress and was sniffing in an exploratory way
around his ankles.

'Tor – ' Cecile Savoy said imperiously. 'I *must* speak
to you about my contract. I don't want – '

'All right, Cecile.' Tor Torrington turned and took
her arm. 'We'll talk about it in your dressing-room.
We can have a bit of privacy there.'

When Mr Herkimer straightened up, to follow Cecile
and Mr Torrington to the dressing-room, Frances was
surprised to see Twinkle stoop and begin to scratch
Fleur's ears. Almost immediately, she felt guilty at her
own surprise. Why shouldn't Twinkle, despite her
tough exterior, wish to be friends with the Pekinese? A
child and a dog had a classic attraction for each other.
It simply proved that Twinkle was not insensible to
childish things, after all.

'Fleur!' Cecile Savoy halted and called for her pet.
'Fleur! Come!'

With an apologetic wave of the plume that served her
for a tail, Fleur-de-lis gave a final lick to Twinkle's hand
and pattered after her mistress.

Tor Torrington looked back over his shoulder and
sized up the situation instantly. 'Let the dog stay here,'
he said. 'It won't be able to add anything to the
conversation.'

Cecile Savoy hesitated, but an order from someone
even more peremptory than herself was obviously hard
to refuse. (Apart from which, wasn't Tor Torrington
usually referred to as the 'money man' of Herkimer-
Torrington Productions?)

'All right, Fleur. Stay, Fleur,' she commanded. The
Pekinese trotted happily back to Twinkle, ready for
playtime.

'At least – ' Mr Torrington's words drifted back to them – 'she's making friends with *something*. It's a start.'

'Okay' – Twinkle raised her head broodingly – 'Okay. Just you wait.'

CHAPTER IX

Laurenda surfaced in time for tea. Frances had already become aware that Laurenda's sense of timing was not of the best. It was, perhaps, the reason why her own career had foundered on the shoals of Starletdom, while her daughter's had gone on to full Stardom. For her age, Twinkle's timing was superb.

Despite – or, perhaps, because of – her mother's absence from the set, she had sailed through the scheduled scenes at a pace that even had the highly professional Cecile Savoy registering approval. But once Laurenda had reappeared on the set, all that had changed.

'Baby . . .' Laurenda wailed. 'You *still* haven't drunk your milk!'

Twinkle looked up warily. Until then, she had been happily engaged in tossing a crumpled ball of paper for Fleur-de-lis to fetch. Cecile Savoy had developed a diplomatic blindness and deafness to her pet's defection to the enemy, and a temporary peace had reigned over the afternoon's proceedings. It was shattered now.

'Twinkle . . .' Laurenda wailed again. 'How *could* you? You *know* I need my rest! You *know* I'm not well! Why do you have to do all these things to worry me?'

'All right.' Dick Brouder rushed forward, throwing a protective arm around Laurenda. 'Don't let it get to you. You know she's only trying to upset you.' He glared at Twinkle.

'I'm not!' Twinkle glared back. 'Look at that mess!' She pointed at the glass of milk. 'I can't drink that. It's all filthy and disgusting!'

Twinkle had a point. The heavier particles of milk – not quite cream – had congealed into a film on top and some of the dust and dirt of the set had settled on it. It had not quite soured, but certainly the early-morning freshness had departed leaving a world-weary appearance.

'Perhaps a fresh glass – ' Frances suggested tentatively.

'No!' Laurenda shook off the encircling arm and stepped forward. 'Twinkle has pulled this too many times – she's gotten away with too many things. This time, she drinks that milk – or we stay here until she does. Even if it takes all night!'

It was already four o'clock. Under the terms of the Licence from the Borough Authority, Twinkle ought to be off the set at four-thirty. Did Laurenda realize that? Or was Laurenda in on a conspiracy with her daughter to close down the Unit? Perhaps Laurenda had even stronger reasons than Twinkle for wishing to be back in the States as soon as possible.

For the first time, Frances recognized Twinkle's mother as a woman who might have a private life – and wondered about it. How could a woman have a private life and maintain the schedule needed by the mother of an under-age child star? No wonder Laurenda had frequent attacks of unidentifiable illness.

'Places, please!' Dick Brouder moved off behind the cameras. 'Come on, this is the last shot of the day. Let's give it everything we've got,' he pleaded.

Twinkle buried her face momentarily in Fleur-de-lis's coat. The Pekinese wriggled happily, twisting to try to lick Twinkle's face. Twinkle, a professional mind to her make-up, raised her head quickly and gently lowered the dog to the floor.

'Places,' Dick Brouder repeated firmly. 'Places for the last take.'

'Not until you finish it!' Laurenda warned. She turned away and followed Dick Brouder.

'I'm *not!*' Twinkle muttered stubbornly, as Continuity adjusted her costume. 'I'm *not* drinking that *mess!*'

'Oh, God!' Continuity cracked. 'I can't stand another minute of this!' She snatched up the disputed glass, took a deep breath and drained it, gagging only slightly. 'Now, *shut up!*' She glared at Twinkle. 'You don't have to lie. You don't have to say anything at all. Just keep your mouth shut and your mother will think you drank it.'

'But – ' Twinkle looked at Frances.

'*She* won't tell!' Continuity rounded on Frances threateningly, a white circle of milk rimming her mouth.

'You'd better wipe your mouth,' Frances acquiesced meekly.

Twinkle nodded relieved approval to both of them and moved off under the lights. Fleur-de-lis pattered after her for a few steps, but Cecile Savoy's training prevailed and she turned aside as she neared camera range and trotted back to leap into Cecile's chair and await her mistress.

'Thanks.' Continuity accepted the handkerchief Frances offered and wiped her lips. 'I'm sorry,' she began, 'but – '

'Don't apologize,' Frances said. 'I don't blame you.' Both First and Morris Moskva had emphasized that the Continuity Girl was the hardest-working member of the Unit. She was the first to arrive on the set in the morning and the last to leave at night, after spending hours hunched over her typewriter typing out lists of the minutiae of every scene that had been shot, and what would be needed for the next day's shooting. It might be the names of the stars that sold the picture but, if anyone deserved a little extra cossetting on the set, it was the Continuity Girl.

'Thanks,' Continuity said again, with a wan smile. 'I don't like to be downbeat, but this picture is beginning to show all the earmarks of a very difficult production. I wouldn't be surprised if it turned out to be jinxed.'

'Quiet!' The command rang out. 'Quiet on the set!' There a pause to ensure that the command had been obeyed, then, 'All right. Roll them.'

The fringe lights went out, the arcs brightened, there came the sharp snap of the clapperboard, then Twinkle began to speak.

'But, Miss Minchin – '

'Cut!' Dick Brouder said, ten minutes later, for the final time. So far as Frances could judge, it had been a perfect take. The others seemed to feel it also. A hum of approval arose from the watchers as the arcs dimmed and Cecile Savoy and Twinkle moved away from their ⊽ laces.

'Fine,' Dick Brouder endorsed. 'That was great. We're really moving along now. If we can keep going like this, we'll wrap it up well under schedule.' He moved forward, with further private words of cheer for his stars.

Twinkle seemed uneasy, Frances noticed. Despite Dick Brouder's praise, Twinkle was wriggling unhappily, glancing constantly towards the sidelines. She seemed anxious to get away and, when Dick Brouder switched his attention to Cecile Savoy, Twinkle bolted.

'You were wonderful, baby!' She was caught up in her mother's arms. 'You really showed them!'

'Yeah, yeah,' Twinkle said, squirming free. 'Let's get back to the hotel now, huh?'

'You're tired, aren't you, baby?' Laurenda stroked her hair. 'None of these characters ever realizes – ' she appealed to Frances for additional sympathy – 'how much all this takes it out of the *artistes*. They think it's easy. Of course, that's because they've never done it themselves.'

'Yes,' Frances agreed abstractedly, wondering why Twinkle was watching Cecile Savoy so intently.

'*And* you've drunk all your milk, like a good girl,' Laurenda crooned. 'Now, why don't you go into your dressing-room and lie down for half an hour or so? I've still got to get a few things seen to – '

'No! I want to go *now*!' Twinkle snarled.

'I'm not quite ready yet, baby,' Laurenda said patiently. 'If you don't want to lie down, why don't you sit down and have another stick of gum and – '

'I don't *have* any more gum,' Twinkle said. 'I want to go and get some more.'

'More?' Laurenda seemed startled. 'But, honey, you

had four packs this morning. I bought them for you myself.'

'Well, I used them all,' Twinkle defended. 'I – I was nervous – ' She groped for an explanation. 'All this stuff – it really takes it out of me.'

'Sure it does, baby.' Laurenda shot a triumphant look at Frances. 'That's just what I've been saying.'

'So, let's go *now*!' Twinkle whined.

Cecile Savoy had finished her conversation with Dick Brouder and was moving towards the chair where Fleur-de-lis waited rapturously to greet her.

Twinkle quailed visibly. 'Let's get out of here,' she said.

But it was too late.

Cecile Savoy had had a fine soprano in her heyday and it was still powerful as it vibrated in a series of rising shrieks that tore through the atmosphere. Half an octave higher and she would have shattered the arc lights. As it was, all the lighter-weight props on the set quivered. So did every human being within earshot.

'Cecile! Miss Savoy! Cecile!' People came running from all corners of the set, converging on the source of the screams. 'What's the matter? Are you all right?'

Surrounded by an audience, Cecile Savoy took a deep breath and her screams reached new heights. A boom camera quivered and had to be dollied back hastily.

'Cecile, darling, what's wrong?' Mr Herkimer was quivering too. He and his partner had come racing across the set from their office.

'All right, Cecile,' Mr Torrington said. 'What is it?'

'Fleur-de-lis! My beautiful little Fleur! She's ruined! Destroyed!' Cecile Savoy held out the Pekinese, which was yelping merrily at being the centre of attention. Fleur seemed far from destroyed or ruined – although she appeared to be attached to her mistress by strange dun-coloured strands, rather like sticky umbilical cords.

Filled with foreboding, Frances ventured nearer. She glanced back over her shoulder, but both Twinkle and Laurenda had disappeared.

'The dog looks all right to me,' Tor Torrington said, unfeelingly. 'What's the matter with it?'

'Matter? Matter?' Cecile Savoy gave fresh evidence that she could have been a magnificent tragedienne had she not opted for the lighter side. 'Just *look* at her!'

'She looks all right to me.' Tor Torrington bent closer and inspected the Peke, who met him halfway. They remained nose-to-nose for a moment, then Tor straightened. 'Smells a bit pungent,' he said. 'Peppermint, I think.'

He extended a tentative hand, dodging past the welcoming wet nose, and let it settle on Fleur's back. 'She's sticky,' he announced. He lifted the hand to his own nose. 'And *that's* what smells of peppermint.'

'It's gum!' Cecile Savoy declared.

'Gum!' Mr Herkimer echoed dismally. He looked around and did not seem surprised at the absence of the one he was looking for.

Gum. Frances stared at the hapless Fleur-de-lis, who was quite unaware of her predicament. Her matted plume waved contentedly and she accepted being the focus of all eyes as merely her due. She yelped again complacently. *Four packs of gum.*

'Ruined!' Cecile Savoy mourned. 'Ruined!' She might have been mourning a convent-educated daughter, now lost for ever.

'Scissors!' Mr Herkimer diagnosed, his enthusiasm in solving a problem triumphing over his tact. 'They're the only way. My daughter by my second wife got her hair full of the stuff once. There was nothing else the hairdresser could do. She was the first girl in the neighbourhood with a crew-cut.'

He met Cecile Savoy's steely gaze and seemed to realize that he had been less than diplomatic. 'Well, that was years ago, of course. Maybe a vet would know of something – '

'Ruined!' Cecile Savoy repeated with finality. 'It will take *ages* for her fur to grow out properly again. And I'd planned on showing her at Cruft's next year.'

'Look on the bright side,' Mr Herkimer pleaded. 'At least, the dog is still healthy. It will just *look* lousy for a few months.'

Cecile quelled him with a glance. 'I shall report this to Equity!' she thundered. 'I shall insist that disciplinary action be taken. Where is that little brat – ?' She looked out over the assembled crowd, searching for the culprit who had long since fled.

'Now, take it easy, Cecile.' Mr Herkimer was quivering again. 'You don't want to drag Equity into this. It's only a childish prank.'

'Childish prank! It was deliberate malice! Against my poor, innocent Fleur – ' For a moment, Cecile Savoy was incoherent with rage. Tor Torrington used that moment to take her by the arm and lead her off the set.

'There's no time to be lost, Cecile,' his firm voice carried back to the others. 'We must get her to a vet at once – before that stuff hardens any more. We can deal with the problem of Twinkle later.'

'All right, folks,' Dick Brouder said flatly. 'That's it for today. Be on hand first thing in the morning.' He turned and walked off the set dispiritedly.

'If there *is* a morning.' The murmur was untraceable, but obviously gave the general opinion. The technicians silently began closing down for the day.

As Frances left the set, she heard the lonely rattle of the Continuity Girl's typewriter begin somewhere in the distance behind her.

CHAPTER X

'Frances, *dear*,' the voice on the telephone said warmly. 'I realize it's terribly short notice, but we were wondering if you could possibly come to dinner tonight? It's just a small party but – '

'I'm sorry,' Frances said, struggling to identify the voice. 'I'm very busy these days. Perhaps another – '

'But, Frances,' the voice wailed, 'we were *so* hoping you could come. We were *counting* on you.' The voice changed and became peremptory. 'I *do* think you ought to come.'

'I'm sorry,' Frances surrendered. 'Who *is* this?'

'Frances!' A shock wave travelled along the wires. 'It's *me* – Amanda. Your daughter-in-law.' In case there should be any doubt remaining, she added, 'Simon's wife.'

'I'm sorry, dear. I couldn't hear your voice clearly.' Mendaciously, Frances threw the blame on to the telephone connection. 'It's a very poor line, isn't it?'

'Just the same, I *do* think you might have known me,' Amanda grumbled, her ego obviously badly bruised. 'I'm the only daughter-in-law you have.'

'I'm sorry,' Frances apologized again. 'I simply wasn't thinking about you – I mean – ' she added hastily, before Amanda could take further umbrage, 'I couldn't place the voice. I'm meeting so many new people these days, and hearing so many different voices – '

There was also the fact, although she did not add this, that the content of the conversation, as well as the voice, had been completely unfamiliar. Her daughter-in-law had never seen fit to invite her to a dinner-party before.

'Yes, we read in the papers that Twinkle had arrived and that filming had started.' Amanda's voice was elaborately casual. 'We'd thought you might ring us, or come over.'

'Why?' Frances asked blankly. Amanda had never encouraged the idea of ringing her up – far less dropping in.

'Why, to tell us all about it,' Amanda said. 'We *are* your family, after all.'

'Oh yes,' Frances said, light beginning to dawn. Amanda was a snob and now, for the first time, her mother-in-law had become a potential social asset and was, therefore, worth cultivating. But Amanda had never been a confidante, and it was a bit late for her to try to become one now. Apart from which, Frances discovered in herself a curious reluctance to betray the problems of the Film Unit. It seemed that a new set of loyalties was being established.

'But you *will* come to dinner tonight, won't you?'

Amanda cajoled. 'Now that you know it's *me*?'

'I'm sorry, dear,' Frances said. 'But I'm not working regular hours – I can never tell what time I'll be getting away. Perhaps some other time. After this job is over – ' She found that she did not wish to contemplate such a time.

'Yes . . .' Neither, it seemed, did Amanda. 'But I *hope* we'll see you before *that*.'

'I'll try,' Frances temporized. 'But I must leave for the Studio now. I'm supposed to be there when Twinkle arrives. So, if you'll excuse me – ' She rang off while Amanda was still assuring her of complete understanding.

'There you are, Frances.' Mr Herkimer hurried forward as she arrived on the set. 'Good. We've been trying to get you, but your phone was busy.' He looked at her accusingly. 'It was out of order, maybe?'

'No,' Frances said, 'I was talking to someone.' He looked at her expectantly, but she did not elaborate. It would have sounded dull in this atmosphere to admit that she had only been talking to her daughter-in-law.

'Ah, well.' After a long moment, Mr Herkimer sighed and admitted defeat. 'You're here now. *And* ahead of Twinkle – which is why I wanted to talk to you. You're going to have to take care of her all by yourself today. Do you think you can manage all right?'

'Yes, I can manage, I suppose.' Frances was startled. 'But what about her mother?'

'Laurenda's sick again.' Mr Herkimer twitched an eyebrow meaningfully. 'We've sent the company car to pick Twinkle up at the hotel and she ought to be here any minute. I'm glad you got here ahead of her.'

'You mean – ' Frances was still shocked – 'that Laurenda is going to let Twinkle come on the set alone? After yesterday?'

'Well,' Mr Herkimer shrugged. '*You're* here.'

It wasn't the same and Mr Herkimer knew it. No wonder Twinkle was so aggressive – she had learned that no one else was going to stand up for her. She was on her own and she had to fight her own battles. It must have been a grim lesson for a child to learn.

'It's not the same,' Frances said.

'Maybe not.' Mr Herkimer shook his head. 'But Twinkle is wearing everybody out. Maybe you'd be doing her a favour if you could make her realize it. The way things are now, everybody is just waiting for the Awkward Age to set in. Yes, even me – ' He raised his eyes prayerfully.

'The minute it starts, she's finished. Just let her teeth or her tits start to stick out,' he said, with relish. 'Just let her shoot up taller than her leading man – and that's it.' He smiled beatifically. 'She's finished!'

'Do me a favour, Herkie.' Unnoticed, Twinkle had come up behind them. 'Hold your breath while you're waiting.'

'Ah, there you are, my little darling.' Mr Herkimer made a quick recovery. 'Sweet as ever.'

'Where's the Director?' Twinkle ignored him, looking across the set anxiously. 'Isn't Dick Brouder here today? If he isn't, I'm going straight back again.'

'I'm here,' Dick Brouder said grimly, appearing as silently as Twinkle had. 'You needn't worry.' He stood over her. 'Open your mouth.'

'Listen, you don't have to act like that – '

'*Open your mouth!*' he thundered.

Momentarily subdued, Twinkle opened her mouth.

'*Wider!*' He bent forward and stared into it. 'All right.' He straightened up. 'Now open your bag.'

'You don't have to – ' Twinkle began to back away. Dick Brouder followed her relentlessly.

'*Open that bag!*'

'There's nothing in it.' Reluctantly, she opened her bag and let him examine it. There was quite a lot in it, but not what he was searching for.

'All right.' He straightened as far as eye level with her. 'Now understand this. Gum is barred from this set. Today and for the rest of the shooting. If once – even once – I catch your jaws moving and there isn't dialogue coming out of your mouth, I'll have you up before Equity faster than Cecile Savoy would.'

'All right for you, Brouder.' Twinkle's small face was so pinched and hate-filled it was hard to believe that it could register the famous winsome charm when the cameras were trained on it. 'I'll hate you for ever and ever!'

'You already do,' Dick Brouder said cheerfully. 'Now, for your next scene, you're going to apologize to Cecile Savoy.'

'I won't!' Twinkle was aghast. 'You can't make me!'

'I can and I will.'

'I'll tell my mother,' she threatened.

'You do that little thing,' Dick Brouder said grimly.

Frances suddenly wondered whether there had been more than one reason for Laurenda's absence today. By her 'illness' she had not only avoided the unpleasantness of an encounter with the outraged Cecile Savoy, she had also avoided the danger of a confrontation with the powers-that-be. Whatever the day might hold in store, Laurenda could not be blamed for any of it.

'I'll fix you!' Defeated, Twinkle fell back on the only one she could depend on – herself. 'I'll – '

'You'll get to your dressing-room and change.' Dick Brouder cut off her threats. 'And hurry up – you're delaying the shooting.'

'I don't care,' Twinkle muttered, but she began to move away.

'Get into your costume,' Dick Brouder ordered. '*And* – he pressed his luck recklessly, 'drink your milk. It's on the dressing-table waiting for you.'

Across the set, Frances saw Cecile Savoy start out of her own dressing-room, carrying a rather moth-eaten Fleur-de-lis. Curiously, Cecile Savoy hesitated in the doorway as she saw them, then turned and retreated into her dressing-room.

'Here we are – ' Frances swung open the door of Twinkle's dressing-room. The glass of milk, as threatened, stood on the dressing-table facing them. Twinkle balked.

'In we go – ' One hand firmly between Twinkle's shoulder-blades, Frances propelled her forward and shut the door.

'I'm not going to drink *that*!' Twinkle was determined to take a stand on something.

'Very well.' Frances allowed her to win. 'No doubt Continuity will oblige again. It isn't all that important.'

'No, it isn't.' Twinkle seemed surprised at this endorsement of her own sentiments. She looked at Frances thoughtfully, as though about to say something else, but the moment passed and she turned away again.

'They're waiting on the set,' Frances reminded her when, after another long pause, Twinkle had made no move towards changing into her costume. 'Let me help you – '

'No!' Twinkle struck down the proffered hand and backed away. 'I can get dressed by myself. I'm not a little kid.'

'Of course you're not,' Frances agreed, remembering when Rosemary had gone through this stage. 'But everyone needs help with buttons and zippers sometimes, so – '

'No!' Twinkle backed farther away, clutching protectively at her neckline, but not before Frances had glimpsed a grubby shoulder-strap precariously secured by a safety-pin.

It seemed that Laurenda could not overcome her invalidism enough even to care for her child's clothing – or to see that anyone else did. Once again, Frances was swept by a feeling of sympathy for the beleaguered Twinkle. How much else was lacking in her young life, despite her lucrative contracts and her name in lights?

'You don't have to hang around,' Twinkle snapped. 'I can take care of everything by myself.'

'I'll wait outside.' Tactfully, Frances gave in. 'If you need any help, just call.'

'Yeah,' Twinkle said. 'You do that.' She walked to the door with Frances and shut it decisively. Frances heard the faint surreptitious turn of the key in the lock. Surely, that was a bit excessive? She had no intention of trying to force her way in where she was not wanted. Of course, Twinkle had no way of knowing that. Perhaps privacy was a luxury she had always had to fight for. Laurenda seemed so unduly preoccupied with

herself as to be unheeding of any niceities or courtesies
due to others.

It was not her problem, Frances reminded herself.
She was merely Twinkle's chaperone for the duration of
the filming. It was not up to her to pinpoint Laurenda's
failings as a mother – even supposing that, having
pinpointed them, she could do anything about them.
But she found her sympathies increasingly with
Twinkle.

A muted uneasiness seemed to be growing on set.
Frances looked around, but could discover no visible
cause. The set was quiet – almost deserted. Or was that,
in itself, a cause?

Surely others ought to be on duty. Not necessarily
standing about waiting for Twinkle, but somewhere in
the vicinity, ready to come forward and take their
places for the next scene. But there was no one behind
the cameras, no one on the lights, not even the Continuity Girl was in sight.

Most especially, Cecile Savoy was still behind her
closed dressing-room door. Was she waiting – were
they all waiting – for Twinkle's apology before the
business of the day could begin? Even Dick Brouder had
disappeared. Where had everyone gone?

And then, from behind the locked dressing-room door
Twinkle's voice rose in a crescendo of screams which
sounded as though they would never stop.

CHAPTER XI

Abruptly, the set was alive with activity. Dick Brouder, Ilse Carlsson and the Continuity Girl materialized from a darkened corner and converged upon Frances, along with Sparks, Props, First, Mr Herkimer, and a host of lesser lights.

'What is it?' Mr Herkimer demanded. 'What's the matter now? Trouble, always trouble.'

'I don't know.' Frances twisted the doorknob ineffectually. 'She's alone in there. There can't be anything wrong. She was all right just a minute ago.'

'She's screaming for her health, then?' Without waiting for an answer, Mr Herkimer began pounding on the door. 'Twinkle,' he shouted. 'Twinkle, sweetheart, let me in. It's Herkie. He'll take care of everything. Let Uncle Herkie in.'

The screams continued unabated.

'Twinkle – ' Frances called. 'Twinkle. Let us in. We can't help you if you won't let us in.'

Still the screaming went on, hysterical and out of control. It was doubtful that Twinkle was even aware that help was near at hand.

'Twinkle, darling – ' Mr Herkimer began.

'Stand back!' Dick Brouder said grimly. He raised his foot and crashed the heel against the lock. Once, twice – the door shuddered. The screaming did not stop.

Once more – and a splintering sound signalled that the wood surrounding the lock was giving way. A final time – and the door burst open and they surged into the dressing-room.

Twinkle stood in front of the full-length mirror, her hands over her eyes, her screams still reverberating through the room.

The others halted just inside the door and stared at her unbelievingly.

The Victorian costume, which had been a perfect fit yesterday, was now sizes too small for her. The ankle-length skirt was at mid-calf and the full-length sleeves reached just below her elbows. It looked as though Twinkle had grown more than a foot overnight.

For once in her life oblivious of an audience, Twinkle stood in the centre of her dressing-room and screamed.

'It's impossible!' Ilse Carlsson gasped. 'Utterly impossible!' She darted forward and seized the hem of the costume she had designed and inspected it closely. Twinkle continued screaming.

'It's all right,' Frances soothed. She and the Continuity Girl had moved forward together. 'It's all right.'

'Here – ' Continuity had taken the glass of milk from the dressing-table. 'Have some of this. Your throat will be raw with all that screaming.'

Either Frances's soothing words, or Continuity's common sense, seemed to get through to Twinkle. The screaming died to a whimper, she kept her hands over her eyes, but she sipped at the milk Continuity held to her lips.

'It's a joke.' Ilse Carlsson straightened slowly. 'It must be. Look, Twinkle – ' She pulled Twinkle's hands away from her eyes. 'The hem has been taken up, and the sleeves have been shortened. You can see – someone did it very quickly using a basting stitch. It wasn't meant to stand up to any sort of close inspection. It was just some sort of joke.'

'Not a very funny one,' Frances said tartly. The 'joke' had been a body blow at Twinkle's deepest fears: of the inevitable, inexorable process of growing up, of losing her childish charm, with the consequent loss of income, employment, status and any sort of future. No wonder she had not been able to stop screaming.

Beginning to realize that a cruel trick had been played upon her, Twinkle fought to control her hysteria. Half-whimpering, half-sobbing, she clung to Frances, as though trying to hold on to normalcy, to childhood, to the life she knew.

'It's quite all right,' Ilse emphasized. She pulled the running thread free and shook down the turned-up hem. 'You see, it fits. You have not changed. The costume has not changed. It is just someone's silliness.'

Someone's silliness. Someone's unfunny joke. Someone's . . . revenge?

The thought seemed to catch at several minds simultaneously. Lifting her own head and looking around, Frances saw other heads begin to lift and turn.

One person was conspicuous by her absence. Only Cecile Savoy had not come rushing to discover the cause of the uproar. Because she already knew?

Once again, in her mind's eye, Frances saw Cecile Savoy start out of her dressing-room, hesitate in the doorway and move back into the room, closing the door behind her. *Because she had seen Twinkle heading for her own dressing-room? Because she knew what was waiting for Twinkle in that dressing-room?*

'I'm okay now.' Twinkle, who had been absently

sipping the milk held to her lips by Continuity, pushed the glass away. She glanced around at the anxious faces and grinned wryly.

'I guess I don't have to apologize to Cecile Savoy now, do I?' she asked Dick Brouder.

'We'll let it go . . . this time.' He obviously saw little to smile about. 'But, if either of you try anything else . . .' He allowed the threat to tail off, possibly because he could think of nothing dire enough to threaten.

'All right.' Mr Herkimer moved forward and took Twinkle by the chin, tilting her face upwards. 'Fine,' he approved. 'You didn't cry and spoil your make-up. We can get on with the shooting.' He looked at Dick Brouder.

'Not with *her*.' Twinkle drew back.

'Perhaps not.' Dick Brouder looked across the set to Cecile Savoy's dressing-room. Tor Torrington was emerging. He met Dick's gaze and shook his head, closing the door behind him with a certain finality.

'It appears that Miss Savoy has decided to take the rest of the day off,' Dick Brouder interpreted. 'Where's Julian Favely – ?'

'Here!' Julian Favely pushed to the front of the crowd. 'Look here, you mustn't blame Cecile. You must admit she's had a great deal of provocation – '

'Right!' Dick Brouder cut him off decisively. 'We'll shoot the scene with Ram Dass next.'

'Equity . . .' Mr Herkimer moaned faintly. 'I'll report them *both* to Equity. I'll take *everybody* to Equity. It shouldn't be allowed. Somebody's got to protect a poor, defenceless producer . . .'

'There now, there.' Ilse Carlsson continued smoothing the sleeves down over Twinkle's wrists. 'There, you see. It is all right.' She appeared to be speaking to the rumpled cloth as much as to Twinkle.

'We'll take the scene where you come over the roof-tops – ' Dick Brouder turned to Julian Favely. 'No dialogue. You just slip over the rooftops, Twinkle opens her window and lets you in. You can handle that without a rehearsal, can't you?'

Julian Favely looked at the mock-up of Victorian rooftops built along in front of a catwalk and went slightly green under his swarthy make-up. 'No trouble at all,' he said airily. If he could act half as well as he could lie, he obviously had a brilliant future ahead of him.

'That's the spirit!' Mr Herkimer brightened. 'We don't want to lose a day's shooting. You can go on with the show, can't you?' he asked Twinkle.

'I don't have to go up there, do I?' Twinkle eyed the catwalk dubiously. 'I might get dizzy.'

'No, no,' Mr Herkimer said expansively. 'We'll shoot you down here on the floor, in the nice little attic room over there. Only Julian goes up on the roof today. He'll come out of that window up there, slide across the sloping rooftops – '

Julian looked, if anything, rather greener. Frances wondered if he might have a dizzy spell.

'We'll shoot him from several angles as he crosses, and then we'll cut to the camera down here behind you as you step back from the window and let him in. When we print it, it will look as though it all happened on the same level.'

'Well . . . all right,' Twinkle said grudgingly. 'But I'm not going up there.'

'No, no, certainly not.' Mr Herkimer managed to

look as though such an idea had never invaded his mind. 'And when you *do* go up, we'll have a nice little safety-harness on you so that nothing can go wrong, even if – God forbid – something goes wrong.'

'What about me?' Julian asked, as Twinkle went to work on untangling Mr Herkimer's reassurances. 'Where's my safety-harness?'

'You don't need one, my boy.' Mr Herkimer slapped him on the back. 'Sure-footed as a mountain goat. This will be child's-play to you. Didn't your agent tell me you used to do mountain climbing?'

'No,' Julian said tersely.

'*I'm* not going up there today or any other day,' Twinkle announced coldly.

'We'll worry about one day at a time!' Tor Torrington had come up behind them. Oddly enough, he did look worried. Perhaps he was afraid that Cecile Savoy had walked off the set for good.

Taking advantage of Twinkle's preoccupation, Continuity had thrust the glass of milk to her lips again and Twinkle had taken several more sips before realizing what she was doing and thrusting the glass away.

'I don't want that junk!' Twinkle protested.

'That's all right.' Dick Brouder was prepared to make a concession. 'You've nearly finished. No more milk till tomorrow now.' He looked at the group still milling around in the dressing-room.

'All right,' he ordered. 'Let's get to work.'

Next morning, unsure of Laurenda's state of health, Frances reported directly to the hotel suite. Twinkle seemed glad to see her although, in what Frances was coming to recognize as her usual way, she tried to hide the fact.

'Oh, Frances, thank heavens you've come!' Laurenda was more forthcoming. 'Now both of us can travel down with Twinkle today, and you can keep her safe in case anything happens to me. I'm not feeling at all well. I wonder if, maybe, it's the water? It's got a funny taste.'

'It's hard water, that's all,' Frances said. 'It's perfectly safe.' As would Twinkle have been, even by herself in the company car. Laurenda had not worried about sending her off alone yesterday.

The telephone rang just then. Laurenda answered and did not appear happy with what she heard. 'The car will be late picking us up,' she complained to Twinkle. 'It seems they picked up Cecile Savoy first and took her down. But there was a delay and they won't get here for a while yet.'

'They took her down ahead of *me*?' Twinkle's eyes narrowed dangerously. 'But *I'm* the Star.'

'Cecile Savoy has to be on the set ahead of you,' Frances reminded her.

'Who told you so?' Twinkle appeared to have been struck by a new thought. One which sharpened her face and shadowed the feral features. '*Who* was it?'

'Why, I believe it was First,' Frances said, startled. 'He was kind enough to explain the regulations about children appearing in films – ' She broke off, realizing abruptly that Twinkle had not been addressing her.

'*Who?*' Twinkle insisted, glaring at her mother. 'Who was it on the telephone? Who?'

'Why . . . why, baby . . .' Laurenda backed away from the seething fury confronting her.

'*Who?*'

'It . . . it was the Director . . . that's all . . .' Laurenda had backed up against the wall and she cringed there. 'Only the Director . . .'

'It was Dick Brouder – that's who!' Twinkle quivered with fury. '*Dick Brouder!*'

'Well, he *is* the Director, baby – '

'That does it!' Twinkle snarled. 'You're not coming with me today – you're staying here!'

'But, Twinkle – ' Her mother began an automatic protest, clearly without any real hope of being allowed to finish it. She halted even before Twinkle cut in.

'You're staying here!' Twinkle ordered. 'Besides – ' she cast a quick sideways look at Frances, as though suddenly remembering her presence. 'I need some new clothes. A skirt and a couple of tops – *you* know. I haven't got time to look for them myself. You'll have to find them for me.'

'I guess you're right.' Laurenda surrendered like one long accustomed to losing, who only put up a brief initial battle for the sake of appearances.

'Frances can take care of me okay.' Twinkle was prepared to be magnanimous in victory. 'Can't you, Frances?'

'Quite possibly,' Frances said dryly. It occurred to her that Twinkle was about as much in need of care and protection as a sabre-tooth tiger – that is, back in the era before sabre-tooth tigers became extinct.

'Sure, you can,' Twinkle said. It was obvious that she, too, thought Frances redundant. She could look after herself better than anyone else could. The jungle was her natural habitat.

Frances surveyed her critically. *Had* Twinkle grown –

just slightly – since yesterday? Not to the grotesque extent that Cecile Savoy's altering of her costume had suggested, but – just *slightly*?

'What's the matter?' Twinkle asked abruptly, alert to the faintest hint of criticism in the air.

'Nothing.' Once again, Frances was conscious of the knife-edge Twinkle balanced on. Twinkle, who had alienated so many people during the brief course of her career, who was surrounded by so many ill-wishers ready to cheer should she plunge forward into disaster.

'So, okay.' Twinkle still regarded her uneasily, as though conscious of unsaid things hovering in the air. She seemed about to ask another question but, before she could formulate it, the telephone rang again.

'Yes? Hello?' Laurenda sprang to answer it, with more animation than she had shown yet. Her troubled face cleared as she heard the message relayed from the other end.

'Oh, fine,' she said enthusiastically. 'That's just lovely. Thank you so much.' She replaced the receiver and turned to face her daughter.

'It's all right, baby,' she said. 'The car is downstairs right this minute. You and Frances can get along now.'

CHAPTER XII

'She isn't coming!' Twinkle said, stepping out of the limousine and sweeping past Dick Brouder in a manner curiously reminiscent of Cecile Savoy's.

Dick Brouder stared after her, flexing his fingers unconsciously. His gaze seemed to focus on her neck.

'Laurenda had to stay in London to do some shopping today.' Frances tried to smooth over Twinkle's rudeness. 'Twinkle needs some new clothes.'

'Twinkle needs – ' Dick Brouder broke off and smiled tautly at Frances. 'Right,' he said. 'We'll try to get that scene between her and Cecile done today. If you'll check with Ilse and Continuity on costume details, I'll get Twinkle rehearsing it.'

He walked off jauntily. Of course, the scene was going to have to be shot some time – and more than one remaining scene called for Twinkle and Cecile Savoy to appear together. It was probably as well to get them back to work as soon as possible. But Frances had the feeling that Dick Brouder was going to enjoy Twinkle's discomfiture today.

In the event, all went smoothly. In her way, Twinkle was as much of a professional as Cecile Savoy in hers. And the antagonisms bristling just beneath the surface were, as Morris Moskva had prophesied, all to the good where the script was concerned. Miss Minchin and Sara Crewe faced each other, crossed swords, thrust, parried, and – when the scene was over – the entire technical crew burst into spontaneous applause, the rarest and highest accolade film stars could achieve.

Cecile Savoy bowed to the assembled technicians and – after a fractional pause – to Twinkle, in the best curtain call manner. Twinkle, after a barely more fractional pause, did the same. She was learning fast and the lessons could only improve her.

Frances saw Dick Brouder and Tor Torrington exchange surprised glances. Evidently, neither of them had thought to see the day when Twinkle would modify her naturally churlish instincts once the cameras had stopped turning.

In a farther corner, Mr Herkimer beamed as though he had engineered the change in her attitude himself.

Cecile Savoy and Twinkle bowed frostily to each other once more and turned away to their separate exits. At least, no one had raised the question of either of them apologizing to the other, and so it seemed they were prepared to ignore the past and begin again. Perhaps, in some odd way, the off-camera scene they had just carried out *was* a mutual apology.

'I was proud of you!' Frances said impulsively, as they entered the dressing-room.

'You were?' Twinkle seemed startled. It was obviously not the sort of remark that came her way often.

'You were really splendid,' Frances insisted. 'You both were.'

'Oh.' Whether it was because genuine praise was so unusual, or because Cecile Savoy had been included in it, Twinkle had an unwonted attack of modesty. 'Well, it was a good scene,' she said. 'It was so good nobody could have loused it up, really, not even if they'd tried.'

'Don't tell me! I can't have heard right!' Morris Moskva, entering the dressing-room behind them, stopped and stared at Twinkle. 'You're not sickening for something, are you? You don't sound like yourself at all.'

'I never said *all* the scenes were good!' Twinkle counter-attacked immediately, but Frances had to admit that there had been provocation. 'Only *some* of them. In fact, maybe that was the *only* one. And that was practically word-for-word from the book.'

'Don't tell me you read the book!' Morris Moskva took a step backwards. 'A whole book? And without any pictures in it, even?'

'I read,' Twinkle said angrily. 'I read a lot more than people think I do. I'm not stupid, you know. Even if I *do* work for Herkimer-Torrington.'

'How did you like the book?' Frances intervened hastily, trying to defuse the situation. 'What did you think of it?'

'Not very much.' Twinkle shrugged. 'It was awfully childish.'

'Yeah,' Morris said. 'I'll bet Harold Robbins is more in your line.'

There was a tap on the dressing-room door and Mr Herkimer burst into the room, preventing another flare-up. 'That was great!' he exulted. 'Now we're really humming. If we can keep on like that, we'll bring this picture in under the budget.'

'*If*,' a dry voice said behind him. Tor Torrington had followed him into the room. It had obviously been Mr Torrington who had thought to knock.

'*If*,' he said again. Tor Torrington, Frances remembered suddenly, was the 'money man' of the production company. And money men had never been famous for taking an optimistic view of anything.

'But it's going well,' Mr Herkimer defended hastily. 'You've got to admit it's going well.'

'Perhaps.' Tor Torrington frowned. It was a warning frown, such as a concerned adult might give to another – more careless – adult who was in danger of lapsing into profanity in the presence of the children. 'But it doesn't do to start counting your chickens before – '

'All right, all right – ' Mr Herkimer waved his hands

in defeat. 'So, we'll hatch them now and count them later.' He nearly knocked over Twinkle's ever-present glass of milk and moved away from the dressing-table before continuing stubbornly, 'But I still say, *if* we can keep going like this, we're in business.'

'We're in business right now,' Tor Torrington reminded him. 'The trick is to ensure that we *stay* in business.' He turned a stern face towards Twinkle.

'You said it!' Twinkle was not to be intimidated. 'This is such a cheap outfit, I'm only surprised you're not doing back-to-back shooting.'

'We might be – ' She had met her match in Tor Torrington. 'If we could have found *two* stories calling for a child star. Scripts are few and far between, you know. You're just a few short steps from being a drug on the market.'

'You're a liar!' Twinkle blanched. 'I'm a Star!'

'*Today* you're a star,' Tor said heavily. 'Tomorrow – ' He did not finish the sentence. He did not need to.

'No!' Twinkle looked ready to hit out. 'No! You're only trying to frighten me!'

And succeeding, Frances thought, noting the pale face, the fists clenched to strike in self-defence. Tor Torrington was certainly no expert in psychology to upset his star just when the filming had begun going so well.

'Tor – ' Mr Herkimer apparently felt the same, he tugged at his partner's arm. 'Tor, why don't you go and play with a trial balance, or something? The *artistes* are my province, remember?'

'Yes, yes.' Tor dismissed Twinkle from his attention. 'But I'm waiting to speak to *you*, remember? We must have a conference – '

'In a minute.' Mr Herkimer waved him away. 'First,

I must congratulate our little star on a magnificent performance, then I must congratulate our script-writer on a magnificently-written scene, then I must congratulate our director – ' He looked about, abruptly realizing that part of the cast was missing.

'He's outside,' Twinkle said, a curious note of triumph in her voice. 'He's with Ilse Carlsson. He's with Ilse a lot.'

'Is he?' Mr Herkimer sent her a look which contained considerably less enthusiasm than the look he had previously bestowed on her. 'Isn't that nice?'

'I guess *he* thinks so,' Twinkle said smugly. 'Do you want to have him paged?'

'I think maybe' – Mr Herkimer said thoughtfully – 'it's time you had a little rest before the next scene. We wouldn't want to tire you out.'

'I'm not tired,' Twinkle said.

'Rest, just rest,' Mr Herkimer said. 'The Regulations say you've got to. So, don't argue – just rest.'

'English rules are stupid!' Unexpectedly, Twinkle whirled on Frances, who was unprepared for battle.

'Perhaps that's because they're framed for English children,' Frances defended as best she could. '*English* children aren't so precocious. They *are* still children, and not – '

She liked to think that she would have stopped there anyway, even if Twinkle's face had not abruptly crumpled. But, before Frances could apologize, Twinkle's mood changed.

'No, *no*, NO!' she shrieked. The hairbrush hit Frances on the temple before she could duck. In rapid succession, it was followed by the hand mirror, the comb, a jar of cold cream –

Half-crouched, arms upflung to protect her head, Frances was dimly aware of the uproar as the others closed in to subdue Twinkle.

'It's all right.' Mr Herkimer had her by the elbow and was gently urging her to her feet. 'It's all right.'

'I'm sorry,' she apologized. 'I didn't mean to set her off like that – '

'If it wasn't you, it would be something else,' Mr Herkimer said resignedly. 'It doesn't take much.' Somehow, Mr Herkimer's arm had insinuated itself around her shoulders. She found that she was leaning against him in a way she had never intended, and recognized that he had pulled her off-balance. 'Why don't we take you home now?' There was no doubt that 'we' meant 'I'.

'No, really,' Frances wrenched herself away. 'It was the suddenness of it – that's all. I can carry on – '

'Of course, you can,' he soothed. He seemed to have grown another hand. It was patting her –

'I'm *quite* all right,' she said firmly, putting some distance between them, and wondering whether she ought to cross the room and attempt to comfort Twinkle now that her temperamental fit had passed.

Twinkle was sobbing quietly, supported by Continuity on one side and Ilse Carlsson on the other. Dick Brouder, too, had made his appearance somewhere along the way and was conversing earnestly with Tor Torrington in a corner.

The dressing-table was swept bare, except for the glass of milk which stood there untouched and untasted. Was it because of Twinkle's repugnance, or simply a natural caution about ruining her costume, which had spared the milk?

Twinkle's face was puffed and streaked with tears, her make-up ruined. Mr Herkimer surveyed her and sighed heavily.

'Bathe her face with cold water,' he directed Frances. 'See if you can get her back into photographic shape.' He was obviously accustomed to dealing with the ravages of temperament. 'Meanwhile, we'll shoot around her.'

'I need some close-ups of Cecile.' Dick Brouder came forward. 'We can go ahead with those.'

'You ought to be taking close-ups of *me*.' Twinkle pushed her comforters away and faced him. 'You can't give anybody more close-ups than me – it's in my contract.'

'You're in no shape for close-ups at the moment.' Dick Brouder eyed her without favour. 'Let Frances wash your face. Then drink up your milk and have a little nap. We'll see what you look like in a couple of hours.'

'I hate you!' Twinkle said.

'We've been over that before.' His voice was heavy with patience.

'And you hate me, too!' There was something sly and mocking in Twinkle's eyes. 'And you can go on hating me, because you're never going to get what you want. Never, never, never!'

'Let's go,' Dick Brouder said to the others. 'She needs her rest, but she's obviously going to keep on performing as long as she has an audience. I'd prefer her acting on-camera.'

They left, following Dick Brouder without a backward glance at Twinkle, who watched them go, her face impassive. Only when Continuity started to leave did she move.

'Wait a minute.' She caught Continuity by the arm, pulling her back. 'You *promised*.' She gestured towards the glass of milk.

'Oh, very well.' Continuity looked around; the others had all gone, the dressing-room door closed behind them. It was obvious that she did not wish to linger. She caught up the glass of milk, drained it at a gulp, grimaced and hurried out.

'She hates me, too.' Twinkle stared after her. 'They *all* hate me.'

'Well, you must admit you haven't been at your most lovable best today.' For want of something to do instead of meeting Twinkle's eyes, Frances took up the milk glass and rinsed it absently in the hand basin.

Silently, Twinkle shouldered her aside and began dabbing at her face with the wash cloth. Frances moved away and sat down in the armchair, not offering to help. Twinkle had a great deal to think about and was best left to herself for a while.

Twinkle finished at the basin and approached the couch reluctantly. 'Do I *have* to have a nap?' she asked.

'It would be better if you did,' Frances said. 'Just lie down and rest, even if you can't sleep.'

Twinkle stretched out on the couch tautly, as though daring sleep to overtake her. She was frowning in thought.

Outside, the normal hum of activity had been going on. Now it stopped abruptly. Unconsciously, Frances tensed, waiting for the screaming to start. There had been silences like that before on this set.

'What's wrong?' Twinkle was on her feet crossing the

room. At the door, she hesitated, as though fearing what she might discover beyond it. Then she opened it.

The screams had never come. Odd, Frances thought, when there was a genuine emergency. Continuity lay slumped on the floor, the others clustered around her.

'She's breathing – ' Cecile Savoy knelt beside her.

'I've rung for an ambulance.' First hurried over to the group. 'It will be here in a couple of minutes.'

'I don't understand it.' Mr Herkimer looked down at Continuity, shaking his head. 'One minute, she was on her feet and just like always – the next minute, she just keeled over. You don't think she's on drugs, do you?'

'Not a chance,' First defended. 'I've worked with her before. She's as straight as they come.'

'Pregnant, maybe?' Mr Herkimer looked around suspiciously. 'That makes them faint.'

'She hasn't fainted.' Cecile Savoy looked up. 'I did ambulance work during the War and I can recognize a faint.' Her gaze crossed First's apologetically. 'She *does* appear . . . drugged.'

'Whatever it is,' Dick Brouder broke in before First could take up the defence again, 'it's put paid to filming for today. We can get along without anyone except Continuity.'

Twinkle drew back into the dressing-room and closed the door. Her face was pinched and wizened. She looked like a little old lady suddenly faced by the inevitability of her own mortality.

'She drank my milk.' Twinkle's voice was a whisper, she might have been thinking aloud. 'That milk was supposed to be for *me*.'

CHAPTER XIII

'You mustn't start imagining things,' Frances said. 'It's probably some sudden virus. The hospital will be able to tell us. By morning, we'll know.'

Twinkle, huddled in a corner of the company limousine, did not appear to be listening. She stared out of the window at the passing landscape, preoccupied with her own thoughts. She had not spoken since leaving the Studio.

Frances, too, had been silent for most of the journey. She had been faintly amused this morning when Laurenda had put such emphasis on Twinkle's safety. Now she wondered how much reason Laurenda might have had for such anxiety. Had there been attempts on Twinkle's safety before? On her life?

Frances stirred uneasily. Surely that was over-dramatizing the situation. Or was it?

The Continuity Girl was a strong healthy adult – a bit on the plump side. And yet, she had suddenly 'just keeled over'. She had not recovered consciousness before the ambulance arrived and, although the ambulance attendants had been cautiously optimistic, had still been unconscious upon arrival at hospital.

What effect would that dosage have had on a small, slender child? Would it have killed her?

'Your hotel.' Both Twinkle and Frances had been so deep in thought that they had not noticed the car pull to a halt. The driver spoke as the doorman opened the car door for them.

'You're back early, baby.' Laurenda, unsurprised but faintly uneasy, greeted them at the door of the suite. 'I've got all your shopping done, though.' She led them into the sitting-room and waved a hand at the garments draped over the back of the sofa.

'Yeah, fine.' Twinkle cast an unenthusiastic eye over the items displayed. They were an amorphous collection of loose and smocked tops, unremarkable skirts and jeans. Frances was rather surprised that Twinkle did not explode in anger at the drab display – but, most probably, the shocks of the day had vitiated her spirit.

'Don't you *like* them, honey?' Laurenda seemed offended by the lack of a positive response. 'I can always change them, if you want, I made sure of that.'

'They're okay.' Twinkle did not give them another look as she headed for her own bedroom wearily.

Laurenda looked at Frances, seeking sympathy for her trials, and seemed surprised when she met with no response.

'Continuity drank my milk again today – ' At the door, Twinkle turned back and faced her mother, radiating an obscure aura of satisfaction. 'Continuity's in hospital now and nobody knows what's wrong with her. She collapsed on the set.'

'No!' Laurenda looked as though she might collapse herself.

'And Dick Brouder told me especially to drink up my milk. Nobody else knew she drank my milk for me – only Frances. Dick said to drink my milk and take a little nap. I wonder, if I'd done that – ' A grim smile underlined her words.

'I wonder if I'd have ever woken up again? Continuity got to hospital because she fell down in a heap. If I'd been lying down anyway, they'd just have thought I *was* taking a nap. They wouldn't have wanted to call me until the very last minute I was needed on the set. I'll bet they'd have had a hard time waking me – *if* they could.'

Twinkle turned and vanished through the doorway.

'Oh, God!' Laurenda collapsed into the nearest chair. 'Oh-God-oh-God-oh-God.' She lifted her head to look at Frances with wan hope. 'Is it true?'

'It's true,' Frances said. 'But it isn't quite the way it sounds. Anyone might have said precisely the same thing to an overwrought child.' But Twinkle's assessment of the situation had been correct. If she *had* fallen asleep, it would have been a long time before anyone would have tried to awaken her. Too long, perhaps.

'Oh, God! I wish I were dead!' Laurenda slumped back in her chair. 'What am I saying? I *am* dead. I've been dead for years. I've been nothing but a walking zombie, and just when I thought maybe – ' She broke off and took a deep breath before continuing. 'I can't stand it much longer. What am I going to *do*? How can I keep going on like this?'

'You mean it's happened before?' Frances was disquieted to find her suspicions seemingly confirmed. 'There have been other attempts on Twinkle's life?'

'No, not that.' Laurenda dismissed Twinkle's peril with a wave of her hand. 'She's always dramatizing. This is probably just her latest idea to get as many people as possible into a lot of trouble and disrupt the whole Unit.'

'But Continuity *did* collapse – '

'No – ' Laurenda was not interested in Continuity's problems either. 'I mean, what's going to happen about *me*?'

Frances began to realize that Twinkle's ego might have been inherited rather than developed by too much attention on film sets. She cast about for something to say but, fortunately, Laurenda did not wait for a reply.

'It's Twinkle this and Twinkle that,' Laurenda complained. 'It's "dear Twinkle" and "poor little Twinkle" and "don't upset Twinkle". But, what I want to know is, what about *me*? Don't *I* have any rights at all? Nobody seems to think I'm entitled to any life of my own. Not even Twinkle – especially not Twinkle! Well, I'm sick of it, I tell you – *sick* of it!'

Perhaps that was why Laurenda seemed so willing to descend into semi-invalidism. Even now, the second wheelchair had not been returned to the hire company, but stood in the foyer of the suite waiting to be utilized again.

'What am I going to *do*?' Laurenda returned to her theme as though she actually thought Frances might be able to supply an answer. 'I can't go on like this!'

'Surely you won't have to for very much longer – ' Frances broke off, remembering that the passage of time was unlikely to be of any more comfort to mother than to daughter. The encroaching years brought more threat than promise to people in their position.

'I mean – ' Frances amended hastily, 'Twinkle is bound to develop more interests of her own as she . . . as time . . .' There was no way to avoid the thought. It had been a mistake to embark on any attempt at comfort.

'By the time Twinkle gets any interests except herself, it will be too late for me,' Laurenda said darkly. 'Twinkle thinks I ought to do nothing except dance attendance on her – day and night. And she's got everybody else thinking the same way.'

'It *is* difficult to bring up a child alone,' Frances said sympathetically, and then realized she might have stumbled into another delicate area. 'You *are* alone?' she asked cautiously.

'Twinkle's father had a brilliant career ahead of him,' Laurenda said. 'So had I – once. When we got married. Then Twinkle was born and things began to get slow in the Industry. Her father got a contract for a spaghetti Western being made in Yugoslavia. The script was lousy, but the money was pretty good, so he thought he'd risk it. There was a good chance it would never get distribution outside Italy, so it wouldn't do his reputation any harm. Besides, a lot of actors were doing it in those days. There was no reason he shouldn't have gotten away with it like the rest of them, but – ' Laurenda shrugged.

'His luck ran out. The second week on location, they were shooting a mine cave-in sequence. The dynamite went off too soon – ' she shrugged again – 'and that was it.'

'There was some insurance, of course. And the film company gave me what they called an *ex gratia* payment. That's spaghetti Western for "hush money", I guess. Anyway, that's what it amounted to. I took the money and shut up. Not that I could do much else. I couldn't afford an international lawsuit, and the company was on the verge of bankruptcy, anyway. Funny thing is, they went on and finished the picture with somebody else and it grossed four million. And they didn't even reshoot the early scenes – where they had Johnnie in long shot – that's how tight a budget they were on.'

Laurenda stared into space, while Frances remained motionless. At this late date, condolences seemed out of place and sympathy had not been invited. Laurenda was simply stating facts, that was all.

'So, there we were.' Laurenda seemed to give herself a mental shake and continued. 'After about a year, I pulled myself together and decided to try to pick up the pieces of my career again. Because I didn't have any money for a baby-sitter, I took Twinkle along with me on an interview. They decided they couldn't use me, but they wanted Twinkle – and that's been the story of my life ever since. I'm typecast as Twinkle's Mother.'

'She's very talented,' Frances offered feebly.

'Oh, sure. She ought to be. I was pretty talented myself – and so was her father. A bunch of real talented people. Maybe, if he'd lived, we could have had our own television series by this time.'

There was no mistaking the bitterness in Laurenda's voice. How much of that bitterness was inner-directed and how much was directed at Twinkle? And how much professional jealousy was involved? It was obviously a highly complicated situation – and new complications were being revealed every day.

'At least, you ought to – '

'I ought to be thankful Twinkle makes enough to support us both, right?' Laurenda finished the sentence in a way that Frances had not intended. 'Sure, that's what everybody keeps telling me. Over and over again. I'm sick of hearing it! Listen, don't you think for one minute that I couldn't get along without that kid. Maybe

I'd get along even better.

'Let me tell you, that kid is a bloodsucker. She's draining the life and energy out of me. Day after day, night after night, *she* wants this, and *she* wants that, and she *doesn't* want – ' Laurenda broke off her tirade abruptly.

'I'm sorry,' she said. 'I'm talking too much. I didn't mean to sound off like that.'

'It's all right,' Frances said. 'I can see you have a lot of problems.' So had Twinkle, if her mother felt this way about her.

'You don't know the half of it.' Laurenda brooded into the middle distance.

The telephone rang. Frances was closer and picked up the receiver. As she said, 'Hello', she heard another click. Twinkle was listening on the extension in her bedroom.

'Good. I was hoping to get *you*, Frances.' Dick Brouder had obviously interpreted the click correctly, too. 'I just wanted to make sure you got back to the hotel safely.'

'We did,' Frances said, nurturing her own suspicions about what he really wanted.

'And Twinkle is okay? She's not upset, or anything?'

'She's all right,' Frances assured him.

'Good. Fine. She's such a sensitive child.' The voice was patently false. 'Well, I'll see you on the set tomorrow. As long as Twinkle is okay. That's all I wanted. He rang off abruptly.

Frances held the line just a trifle longer. Just long enough to hear Twinkle say softly, 'Like hell!' before she hung up.

'Listen – ' Laurenda seemed to have no curiousity

about the call. 'I could manage fine all by myself. I
could get a job – it needn't be acting. I could work
outside. Learn shorthand or something. I could get
along.'

'I'm sure you could,' Frances murmured soothingly.
But could Twinkle? Or was Twinkle being included in
Laurenda's calculations at all?

'I could find a nice little apartment. A smaller place –
I wouldn't need to put up a front any more.'

No, it didn't sound as though Twinkle were being
included.

'I've got enough put by – ' Laurenda looked up then
and caught Frances's eye. 'Oh, now listen,' she protested. 'You *don't* think that! It's my own money, not
Twinkle's. We've got laws in the States about the
earnings of child stars. Ever since a couple of nasty
court cases in the Thirties. The laws were changed to
protect them after that. Half their money goes straight
into a trust to be held for them until they come of age.
The other half can be used for an allowance and for
living and professional expenses – and, believe me,
they're pretty high. You needn't worry – I'm not
stealing Twinkle's earnings.'

Frances had not considered the idea before, but
Laurenda's quick defensiveness raised an interesting
question.

'Just a little place of my own, that's all I want – '
Laurenda had gone back to her brooding. 'Where I can
live my own life. In peace and quiet – '

Perhaps Laurenda couldn't get her hands on
Twinkle's money right now. But, if anything were to
happen to Twinkle, wouldn't Laurenda inherit as next
of kin?

CHAPTER XIV

'How's Continuity?' was Twinkle's first question as they arrived on the set in the morning.

'She's recovering.' Mr Herkimer winced, as though he wished the subject had not been raised. 'They pumped her stomach out and she felt a lot better. She'll be back on the set tomorrow.'

'What happened?' Laurenda was not prepared to let the subject drop either. Pale and wan, she had determinedly accompanied her daughter to the Studio.

'Happened? Happened? What should happen? The silly girl was probably just taking tranquillizers. Everybody takes tranquillizers in the Industry. It's an occupational hazard.'

'*Probably.*' Twinkle pounced on the weak spot instantly. 'You mean you're not sure?'

'She can't talk much yet. And she wasn't feeling strong enough for visitors – '

'You mean you don't *know.*' Twinkle turned away. 'That's what I thought.' She started across the set, followed by her mother.

'Go after her,' Mr Herkimer begged Frances. 'Explain – '

'Explain what?' Frances asked.

'You're against me, too.' Mr Herkimer looked defeated.

'I'm not against anyone,' Frances said. 'I simply don't understand what's going on here.'

'You and me both.' Mr Herkimer sighed heavily,

then recovered himself. 'Why does anything have to be going on? There's been an accident, that's all. Some silly girl took an overdose and didn't have the decency to wait until she got home to collapse. No, she had to go and do it on the set and make trouble for Herkimer-Torrington Productions. As though we hadn't had enough troubles in the past – '

'You mean – ' Frances remembered an earlier remark of his – 'in the Sixties?'

'The Sixties!' Mr Herkimer shuddered. 'Don't talk to me about *them*!'

'But what happened then?' Frances was genuinely curious. 'I don't remember any major upheaval – '

'You wouldn't – it was nothing to you. But, to us, it was a nightmare. Because of the Indies – the independent producers,' he explained. 'They talked a great game. They got legitimate Studios to back their productions. They got big stars to go along with them on percentage deals – you wouldn't believe the names! They wanted *cinéma vérité*, they used hand-held cameras, they filmed on location in the middle of cities – '

'What was wrong with that?' Frances asked.

'Nothing – at first,' Mr Herkimer said. 'At first we thought it was great – even the stars did. And so cheap. Such savings without all those overheads – just like they promised. We thought we'd saved a fortune. And then they moved into the cutting rooms – and we discovered we'd lost a fortune.'

'Why?'

'Because the films couldn't be cut. Those whiz-kid geniuses were so cheese-paring they hadn't allowed any overrun on the scenes. Even for jump cuts, you need a few extra frames that won't cut into the action when you lose them.

'But those Indie directors – nothing! Not an extra frame. And there was no way of getting the cast back together again for more shooting. The actors had dispersed, flown all over the world to work on new pictures – died, even. Whole feature films had to be scrapped because they couldn't be cut together to make sense.

'I tell you, the money Herkimer-Torrington lost – the money all major Studios lost – don't talk to any of us about the Sixties!'

'But you're doing well now, aren't you?' Frances tried to calm him.

'Oh yes, we're back in the black ink again, making profits again. And, believe me, we're going to keep on making profits. That's why both Herkimer and Torrington are over here with this production. We're keeping tighter control these days. And we're not going to let any Continuity Girl make trouble for us either. If she thinks she can sue us, she can forget it. We'll bring in the best lawyers in town to prove it was all her own fault.'

'I'm sure she'd never dream of doing such a thing.' Frances felt it unfair to poor Continuity that her good deed in drinking Twinkle's milk should have had such dire consequences, and then be so misconstrued.

'You don't think so?' Mr Herkimer was eager for comfort.

'Not for a moment.' Frances hoped she was right. It was possible that Continuity *might* have grounds for some sort of lawsuit. Even the hint of one would not reflect well upon Herkimer-Torrington Productions. 'Actually,' Frances added thoughtfully, 'I don't think you ought to suggest such a thing, not even talking between ourselves. It might put ideas – '

'Into the air and, from the air, into her head.' Mr Herkimer finished for her. 'You're right. I never thought of that. I knew you were smart when I hired you. You got a good head on your shoulders.' He gave her a languishing look. 'But two heads are better than one, and maybe someday I can have *my* head on – '

'I really must see how Twinkle is getting on.' It was time for a strategic retreat. 'That *is* what you hired me for, remember?' Before he could reply, Frances slid away.

In the dressing-room, she found Laurenda slumped in the armchair in her usual state of semi-collapse. Twinkle circled the room suspiciously, glaring at each familiar innocent-seeming object as though it might conceal a booby-trap. As, indeed, it might. Twinkle had good reason for her suspicions, as Frances was coming to realize.

There was no glass of milk in view. An oversight? Or a tacit admission that others on the set might have come to the same conclusion as Twinkle?

'You'd better get into your costume, baby.' Laurenda opened one weary eye and closed it again. 'Frances will help you.' It was obvious that Laurenda wouldn't.

Twinkle approached her costume with caution. It was invitingly laid out on the divan and she inspected every hem before shrugging out of her top and jeans and diving into its folds.

'Not so fast,' Frances protested, laughing. 'You'll tear it. You don't have to *fight* your way into it, you know.' Her laughter stopped abruptly as she wondered whether Twinkle were encountering hidden resistance inside the costume: the lining sewn together, perhaps, or pins – long, deadly pins concealed in the inner folds.

'I want to get it over with.' Twinkle's head emerged at the neck of the garment and Frances breathed a silent sigh of relief. No hidden dangers in the costume then – *this* time. She decided that, in future, she would inspect the costumes before Twinkle got into them. Twinkle, acting on past experience, was merely concerned about the hemlines, it had not occurred to her yet that costumes could be put to more sinister use.

Twinkle's hair was tousled and she was breathing heavily, as though she had fought a more dangerous battle than merely struggling too quickly into an unfamiliar costume. Perhaps, after all, Twinkle *had* feared other hidden dangers. The child was quite intelligent.

'I can't reach all the buttons.' Twinkle spun around and Frances began to struggle with the complex arrangement of hooks and eyes and buttons that paraded the back length of the costume.

Laurenda had opened her eyes and was watching apathetically. 'Don't squirm around so much, baby,' she said. 'You're making it harder for Frances.'

'Well, I've got to get comfortable, haven't I?' Twinkle twitched her shoulders and tugged uneasily at the bodice of her costume. 'Something's funny about this – and if it looks the way it feels – '

'It looks fine,' Laurenda said sharply. 'Just quit pulling at it or you'll ruin it and everybody will get upset.'

'*I'm* upset!' Twinkle declared. 'Let them worry about *me*. If I get any more upset, maybe I'll walk off the set – for good.'

'Now, you know you don't mean that, honey.' Laurenda was instantly placating. 'This is a great picture. It will do a lot for your reputation – for everybody's reputation. A lot of nice people have an awful lot riding on this picture. You wouldn't want to hurt them, would you?'

'*Some* of them I wouldn't mind,' Twinkle said darkly. '*Some* of them I wish would drop dead.'

'Baby! You'll shock poor Frances!'

'Will I?' Twinkle glanced at Frances unbelievingly.

France tried to meet her gaze levelly and not show the shock she had felt. The shock had nothing to do with Twinkle's childish rebellion, and everything to do with the expression which had flashed briefly across Laurenda's face as she spoke to her daughter.

Twinkle had had her back turned and had not noticed. Now that Frances came to think of it, Twinkle did not look directly at her mother often. Was it because she knew the expression she might see on her mother's face?

'Ready in there?' First rapped on the dressing-room door and flung it open. 'Everything all right?'

'I'm coming.' Twinkle moved forward after a final twitch at her costume.

In the distance Frances saw a small figure of approximately the same size and colouring as Twinkle move swiftly away from the chalk lines in front of the cameras.

'Who's that?' Twinkle saw her, too, and stopped dead, frowning. 'What's *she* doing on the set? You know there aren't supposed to be any kids on the set but me. It's in my contract.'

'Come off it, Twinkle,' First said wearily. 'You know you've got to have a stand-in. *You* don't want to stand around for hours while they adjust the lights and camera angles, do you?'

He obviously had a point. Equally obviously, Twinkle did not want to admit it. She shrugged and turned away.

'That kid!' First watched her walk across the set to her place in front of the cameras. 'This is the last time I work on one of her pictures. She makes King Kong look like Little Bo-Peep.'

'She's very insecure,' Frances offered in defence.

'She's right to be. She's alienated practically everyone in the Industry. The minute she starts to slip, they're going to queue up to put the boot in.'

And, quite possibly, foremost in the queue would be her own mother. Poor Twinkle. The situation was not without historical precedent, but it was sad.

The stray thought surprised her, although she realized that it was not the first time that it had occurred to her that there was something familiar about Twinkle's plight. But what? Something historical – ? She groped after the flickering memory.

'No, I won't! I won't, *I won't*, I won't!' Twinkle's shriek of outrage cut across the sound stage, driving away all lesser thoughts and preoccupations.

'Twinkle, baby!' Laurenda came bursting out of the dressing-room, startled into animation for once. 'What's the matter?'

'They can't make me!' Twinkle screamed. 'I'll walk off the set! I'll quit the picture! I won't do it!'

Once again, everyone converged on the source of the

screaming, although most of the audience had jaded expressions.

'*Now* what?' Morris Moskva spoke for them. 'What is it this time?'

'They want me to go up *there* – ' Twinkle pointed with horror to the catwalk concealed by mock-ups of rooftops that stretched just below the ceiling of the sound stage. 'They want me to go up there and dance around.'

'You know the dance,' Morris said. 'We rehearsed it with you before you left California.'

'Yeah, but we rehearsed it on the *ground*,' Twinkle said. 'And that's where I'm doing it – or I'm not doing it at all!'

'Now, what's the problem?' First pushed to the front of the crowd. 'That dance is going to be our big production number – you know that. You've known that all along.'

'I didn't know I was going to have to go up there. I thought you were going to fake it with trick photography – and you'd better, because I'm not going up there.'

'*Such* a fuss.' Cecile Savoy was amongst them, holding Fleur-de-lis on a tight rein as the Peke tried to wriggle over to greet her new friend. 'When I played Peter Pan, I had to *fly* out over the audience every night and three matinees a week. And, I may say, I did it without any uproar like this.'

'Okay,' Twinkle said. 'You can do it again, then. Take my part.'

Several people looked as though they wished Cecile could.

'Why not?' Twinkle urged. 'It could be done as a

dream sequence with Ram Dass and Miss Minchin, instead of me. I could be in my room and fall asleep looking out over the rooftops and then Miss Minchin and Ram Dass come on and dance across the rooftops.'

Morris Moskva looked momentarily reflective, then recovered himself. 'Because I wrote it *this* way,' he snapped. 'And I don't let the actors tell me how to write!'

'It *could* work, Morrie,' Laurenda said tentatively. 'You know it could. Twinkle knows a lot about these things, she's been around the Studios all her life.'

'*I* certainly wouldn't mind,' Cecile Savoy said, in the voice of one urging the baby to eat-up-all-the-delicious-strained-goop-or-Mummy-will-eat-it-all-herself-yum-yum.

'Good!' Twinkle fixed her with a basilisk gaze. 'Then you can go right ahead and do it.'

'Perhaps I will.' The lofty disdain of Cecile Savoy's rejoinder was marred as Fleur-de-lis lunged forward to try to leap upon her friend, Twinkle, who was so unaccountably ignoring her. Cecile jerked sharply at the leash, pulling Fleur up short. The Peke yelped in protest, then retreated whimpering to nuzzle unhappily at Cecile's ankles.

'Look, why don't we think this over?' Dick Brouder moved between Twinkle and Morris Moskva, smiling ingratiatingly at both of them. 'Why don't we sleep on it tonight? Then we can decide in the morning which line we'll take.'

'If Twinkle really doesn't want to do it – ' Laurenda began uncertainly.

'I don't!' Twinkle snarled.

'We'll sleep on it, right?' Dick Brouder patted her arm reassuringly. 'Where's the harm in that?'

Laurenda might have been able to answer that question if she put her daughter's welfare first. Or perhaps Laurenda did not consider that Twinkle's fears had any real foundation. And perhaps they hadn't, Frances had to acknowledge.

But Continuity *had* collapsed on set after drinking the milk intended for Twinkle. In view of that, Twinkle's attitude did not seem unreasonable. Why should she be so imprudent as to expose herself to another source of possible danger? It was surprising that any script-writer or director could expect her to.

But they didn't know. Frances remembered belatedly that Morris Moskva and Dick Brouder had no idea of Twinkle's dark suspicions. Nor did they know that Continuity had been in the habit of drinking Twinkle's milk. So far as they were concerned, Continuity had inexplicably collapsed and possibly they would get an explanation from the hospital in due course. Twinkle, of course, was simply being her usual obstreperous self.

Surely Laurenda ought to add her protests to Twinkle's. She was aware of the situation. But Laurenda seemed well on the way to allowing herself to be persuaded over to the Herkimer-Torrington camp.

'Maybe it won't be so bad, baby,' she coaxed. 'They've got a really good little safety-harness, and if you take a tranquillizer and don't look down – '

'I might have known you'd be on *his* side!' Twinkle backed away from Laurenda's outstretched hand.

'Look – ' Dick Brouder said, with false heartiness. 'I'll tell you what we'll do. We're going to think about this overnight, anyway, right? And it's a big number – it will take a few days to shoot. So right now, why don't we just do the opening? That takes place in Sara's attic room, with her looking out of the window and singing the lead-in. Whatever we decide, that will stay the same. So why don't we start with that?' He looked at Twinkle expectantly.

'I don't know . . .' Twinkle appeared to be studying the proposition from all sides, looking for the snags.

'That's right,' Morris Moskva said enthusiastically. 'That bit won't change. We can get that done this afternoon.'

'Come on, baby,' Laurenda said. 'That's fair enough, isn't it? Where's the harm in that?'

'Well . . .' Dubiously, Twinkle allowed herself to be led back on to the set and into camera position.

They had intended to shoot this opening scene all along, Frances realized. The stand-in had been positioned where Twinkle stood now, the lights were all adjusted for her height, the camera angles all marked out. So why had there been all this fuss about a scene that might not be shot for days yet?

'So far, so good.' First breathed a sigh of relief. 'You see,' he explained to Frances's questioning gaze, 'actors are a bit like horses. Before you can break a horse to the saddle and bridle, it's a good idea to show it to him a few times first, and get him used to the idea.'

'Do you really believe Twinkle will get used to *this* idea?' Frances asked.

'Of course. That's the point of the whole exercise. If we'd just sprung it on her the day we intended to shoot – well, you saw what happened. A whole day's shooting, perhaps more, would have been lost. Now that she knows she's got to do it – sooner or later – she'll come to terms with the idea. In another day or two, she'll be up there larking about as though she had her own pair of wings.'

'Mmmm,' Frances said.

CHAPTER XV

When Frances arrived on the set next morning, it seemed deserted. Looking around uneasily, she saw the door to the Production Office standing open. Perhaps Mr Herkimer was to be found in there.

However, there was only Tor Torrington inside, working at his desk. Just as she began to back away, he looked up and saw her in the doorway.

'Come in, Mrs Armitage, come in,' he said. 'I've been meaning to have a little talk with you.'

She had no choice but to enter and take the chair he indicated in front of his desk.

'You seem to be having an excellent effect on Twinkle, Mrs Armitage,' Tor Torrington said approvingly. 'She's much calmer and more amenable these days.'

'She is?' Frances tried not to imagine what Twinkle must have been like on earlier pictures.

'You're worth every penny we pay you,' he assured her solemnly. 'To tell you the truth, Herkie went over the budget allotment in hiring you and I wasn't too pleased at first. But I should have had more faith in Herkie – he was right. Even on a tight-budget picture, there are things it doesn't pay to skimp on – and people are the most important items.'

'Yes.' Frances could not resist adding, a trifle tartly, 'I'd wondered if you had chosen to film *Sara Crewe* because it was in the public domain.'

'Exactly, Mrs Armitage.' He evidently recognized no shade of criticism in her remark. 'We have to pay an enormous sum for a good scriptwriter, who would be needed in any case, so we've saved by not wasting money on what authors call "original material". We've had enough trouble with that in the past.'

'You mean, in the Sixties.' Frances was learning to translate cryptic remarks uttered in that tone of voice.

'Exactly.' He sounded faintly surprised at the extent of her knowledge. 'If you know that much, then you must know that Herkimer-Torrington have been through some long lean years. Oh, the years may seem fat now, but the lean years could come back again and we want to keep production costs down and have a cushion for ourselves next time. That's why we're trying to keep expenses to a minimum.'

'Of course,' Frances murmured dubiously, trying to close her mind to the amount of money the hotel suite must be costing the company.

'You're thinking of the hotel bills – ' Mr Torrington homed in unerringly on her thoughts. 'They'll be high, of course. In fact – ' he winced involuntarily – ' they'll be astronomical. But we want to keep our star happy.'

'I'm not sure that Twinkle really appreciates all that luxury,' Frances said.

'Ah, but *Laurenda* does. Poor Laurenda – she's had her lean years, too.' Mr Torrington sighed. 'We're very fond of Laurenda and we'd do a lot to keep her happy. Even though it's costing us a small fortune – '

Frances interpreted his solicitude as fear that

Laurenda might pull Twinkle out of the picture if her demands were not met, if she were not kept happy.

'Even all the insurance that we carry on Twinkle is just for Laurenda's peace of mind. Not that we begrudge those high premiums for one minute – ' he winced again. 'You can't blame Laurenda. Her husband died working on a picture, you know. It left scars. So we have to over-insure Twinkle to reassure Laurenda. That way, if anything should happen to the child – not that anything ever would – well, there'd be *some* compensation for Laurenda to help her make a new start.'

'I see,' Frances said. She remembered the bitter twist of Laurenda's mouth as she had said "*hush money*" when speaking of the payment she had received after her husband's death. Perhaps it had seemed that way to other people in the Industry, too. So much so that they kept Twinkle well insured to make certain that, if anything should 'happen' to her, Laurenda could be depended upon not to make a fuss.

But perhaps it went even farther than that – perhaps the knowledge of the sum involved was intended to undermine Laurenda's natural concern for her daughter's best interests. Certainly, Laurenda tended to side with the studio, rather than with Twinkle, when disputes arose.

It was a disquieting thought, and brought all manner of other disquieting thoughts in its wake.

'Well, I've enjoyed this little chat with you, Mrs Armitage.' Tor Torrington rose from behind the desk, effectively ending the conversation. 'Drop in again, some time.' He obviously hoped that she would not.

'Thank you,' Frances said, matching him in insincerity; 'Perhaps I shall.'

Frances had scarcely closed the door of the Production
Office behind her when she heard sounds of altercation
nearby. Turning, she saw Continuity looking beleaguered and apparently in the midst of an argument
with Mr Herkimer. With a fellow-feeling for another
sufferer, Frances went over to join them.

'Brave – such bravery – ' Mr Herkimer was saying.
'To have attempted . . . what you attempted – and then
to pull yourself together and come back to face us all
again.'

'I didn't attempt *anything*!' Continuity faced him with
growing fury. 'I don't know *what* happened to me. One
minute I was fine – the next minute I was waking up in
hospital.'

'Ah, women!' Mr Herkimer changed his track
smoothly. 'So brave – with so many obscure little
female things that can go wrong with them. And still
they carry on. Such bravery – such heroism.'

'Nothing "*female*" went wrong with me!' Continuity
disclaimed heroism with raging scorn. 'I don't know
what it was – but the hospital is still running tests. And,
when they find out – '

'Ah! Here's Frances!' With a relieved light in his
eye, Mr Herkimer pounced upon her. Perhaps he was
belatedly remembering her advice not to say anything
to remind Continuity that there were such things as
lawsuits in the world. 'How are *you* this morning? And
how is our little star?'

'She's coming along later,' Frances told him.
'Laurenda rang me and said they'd come down in the
company car and meet me here. She said it wasn't

necessary for me to come to the hotel.'

'That's all right!' Mr Herkimer seemed anxious that she should not think that he was, however subtly, accusing her of any dereliction of duty. 'When Twinkle has her own dear mother with her, what else does she need?'

Quite a bit, Frances would have thought, having seen Laurenda in action – or, rather, in her customary inaction.

'She needs a chaperone, of course.' Hastily, Mr Herkimer tried to retrieve what he felt to be a tactless question. 'She needs *you*, you must never doubt it. You've seen Laurenda – one moment she is fine, the next moment she is ill again. You can never be sure of her, never depend on her.'

'Quite,' Frances said crisply.

'Poor Laurenda – ' Mr Herkimer rushed on, trying to block off what he sensed to be criticism. 'There are problems . . . many problems . . . on both sides. It isn't easy to be a Star. Nor is it simple to be the Mother of a Star. What Laurenda needs – ' He broke off abruptly, as though conscious of an impending indiscretion.

'Quite,' Frances said noncommittally again. She noticed that Continuity had taken advantage of Mr Herkimer's divided attention to slip away.

'Now, I will tell you something – ' Mr Herkimer grasped her arm firmly, before she could slip away. 'Today we are going to shoot that tricky scene. This very morning – before Twinkle has too much time to think it over.'

'She won't like it,' Frances warned.

'She will not even notice it,' Mr Herkimer assured her. 'Laurenda knows which side her bread is buttered on – she will see that little Twinkle gets a nice soothing tranquillizer in her orange juice this morning. By the time we are ready to shoot, Twinkle would be willing to climb up the framework of the Eiffel Tower without a qualm.'

Either he was under a grave misapprehension as to Twinkle's sense of self-preservation, or what the child was being fed was of a strength considerably beyond that of the average tranquillizer. Frances felt a distinct stirring of uneasiness.

'I promise you, it will be all right.' He was quick to sense her disbelief. He made an expansive gesture. 'I guarantee it!'

Pride goeth before a fall, she thought, and instantly wished that she hadn't. The catwalk was so high and Twinkle was so small. It was a long, long way to fall.

'Don't worry.' He patted her arm. 'Everything is going to be all right.'

But someone ought to worry. Mr Herkimer, Dick Brouder and the others on the set had a vested interest in ensuring that Twinkle performed to order. Laurenda ought to worry about her only child, but – quite obviously – was not going to. Twinkle stood alone, a lonely figure, knowing that she was a pawn in everyone else's game, and too young to have a game of her own. No wonder she exploded in temperamental outbursts.

By the time Twinkle and Laurenda arrived, the day had settled down to a steady course. The pale anonymous stand-in vanished as the limousine turned in at the gates, taking no chance this time that Twinkle might catch an unsettling glimpse of her. But the stand-in's work had been done, the lights and cameras were aligned for shooting along the upper level. Twinkle was walking into a trap already baited and ready to snap shut.

But the thought was absurd. Why should anyone want to harm a ten-year-old child? A very valuable child, moreover. Without Twinkle, the picture could not be finished. Hundreds of thousands – perhaps millions – of dollars would have gone to waste.

Or could the picture be finished without her? How good was the stand-in? How closely did she resemble Twinkle? She had never come close enough for Frances to get a good look at her. Was there a facial resemblance as well as a physical one? And was that why Twinkle had become so hysterical about the stand-in?

It was absurd, utterly absurd. Frances clung to that conviction as she watched Twinkle move slowly across the sound stage towards her dressing-room, glancing around suspiciously as though she had scented danger in the supercharged air.

Frances determined to have a private talk with Continuity at the first opportunity and try to find out more about what had happened. It needn't have been an overdose. There were other possibilities. There were tranquillizers which had a deadly effect when mixed with certain otherwise innocent foods like cheese or yeast extract. Perhaps Continuity had been on tranquillizers – which wouldn't be surprising, considering the demanding nature of her job – and had unwittingly eaten a piece of cheese, or something else that didn't mix, and thus collapsed without warning. It needn't have been the milk.

Perhaps she ought to watch Twinkle carefully today

to make sure that she didn't eat a cheese sandwich for lunch, if her mother had succeeded in slipping a tranquillizer into her breakfast orange juice. Not that there was much doubt about that. Frances was beginning to learn that when the Studio spoke, Laurenda jumped – even if Twinkle didn't. And Mr Herkimer had seemed very certain that Twinkle would have had something to put her into a relaxed enough state to do the hated scene.

The sound stage was abnormally quiet; Frances realized the technicians seemed to have disappeared. In the distance, there came a faint sound of barking from Cecile Savoy's dressing-room. Frances was abruptly aware that she was alone on the set. It was as though everyone had gone into hiding, tensed, waiting for some imminent explosion. Or for something to happen with which they would rather not be associated.

Frances crossed quickly to Twinkle's dressing-room, knocked and entered. The semblance of normality inside relaxed her.

It was coffee break, of course. That was where everyone had gone. They would be gathered around the urn in the tiny but fully-equipped kitchen on the far side of the set, probably with the door closed. That was the reason for the silence, the absence of technicians. It undoubtedly happened every day and she simply had not been aware of it because she was usually in the dressing-room with Twinkle at this hour.

'Coffee?' Laurenda held the coffee-pot poised over a cup. Twinkle, Frances saw, had a pot of chocolate all to herself.

'Actually,' Frances fought down a quiver of alarm, 'I

believe I'd prefer some hot chocolate this morning – if
Twinkle can spare it.'

'Be my guest.' Twinkle gave her a strangely blank
look as she passed over the chocolate-pot. Why did
people always speak of Orientals as being inscrutable?
It was children who were the real inscrutables.

'Thank you.' Frances watched the molten stream of
viscous liquid flow into her cup. It *looked* all right.

'Baby – ' Laurenda prodded. 'Shouldn't you be
getting into your costume?'

'I don't want to,' Twinkle said. 'It's different.'

'Don't be silly, honey.' Laurenda studied the depths
of her coffee cup as though looking for some answer
there.

'It *is*!' Twinkle insisted.

'Let me see – ' Frances reached out for the costume
and, after a moment's hesitation, Twinkle handed it
over.

'It *seems* all right.' Twinkle watched her as, frown-
ingly, she inspected the costume. But Twinkle's unease
had infected her. Something was *not* right.

'You're being silly, both of you.' Laurenda poured
herself another cup of coffee, abdicating from the
proceedings.

'Perhaps . . .' Frances let her fingers probe the costume, sliding amongst a curious tangle of inner straps
to emerge unexpectedly in places where there was no
logical reason for a costume to have slits. Unless a
safety-harness had to be attached and accommodated
in some way.

'You see?' Twinkle looked at her anxiously. '*That's*
not the costume I've been wearing all along. It's
different.'

'Yes,' Frances agreed. 'It is.' Her fingers wriggled uncomfortably through the narrow slits. Ought she to say more?

'You're being silly!' Laurenda stuck to her story. (The one she had carefully rehearsed?) 'That's the same costume Twinkle wore yesterday – *and* the day before.'

'No, it isn't,' Twinkle said. 'There weren't any holes in it – then.'

'Look!' Laurenda spoke with unusual decisiveness. 'Either put it on and get on the set, or put it back in the wardrobe and let's go back to the hotel. I don't want to hang around here all day listening to you whine!'

It was unfair. Twinkle had not been anywhere near whining. She was simply an unhappy, puzzled child, faced with circumstances beyond her control. Considering which, she was coping rather well. Frances would not have liked to wager, given a roughly parallel situation, that Laurenda would have behaved nearly so capably.

'Oh, all *right!*' Impatiently, Twinkle snatched the costume away from Frances, nearly breaking a fingernail which caught on the inner tangle of straps. 'I'll *wear* it – but I won't *like* it!'

'That's a good girl.' Laurenda's complacent tone did not entirely conceal her relief.

'Shall I help – ?' Frances started forward.

'*I* can do it!' Twinkle whirled away.

'Why don't you go and see how soon they want to start shooting,' Laurenda intervened with a limp approximation of tact. 'Tell them Twinkle is coming. They must be wondering where she is, by now.'

Twinkle was getting into her costume, making no further fuss and apparently not noticing the curious reinforcement of highly-suspicious strapping. Just how strong were those tranquillizers?

Not strong enough.

'No.' This time, Twinkle wasn't screaming. She spoke with a cold finality that went beyond tantrums and carried more weight. 'I'm not going to do it.'

'Please, baby – ' her mother said.

'According to the terms of your contract – ' Tor Torrington began.

'How *un*professional,' Cecile Savoy shrugged. 'Of course, what else could one expect?'

'I'll report you to Equity,' Mr Herkimer threatened.

'What's wrong with it?' Morris Moskva demanded. 'I'm not rewriting it again!'

They were all drawn up facing Twinkle: the big guns. Discharging their heaviest ammunition, all together and one by one, at the tiny forlorn target facing them unarmed.

'It's a lousy script – that's what's wrong with it!' Twinkle trained her own toy popgun on the one she felt most able to contend with. 'It's nothing but a steal on that Julie Andrews number in *Mary Poppins* – and I bet they didn't make *her* jump around in the rafters twenty feet off the ground!'

'The hell it is!' With the roar of a bull wounded in his professional pride, Morris Moskva charged forward to lock horns in battle. 'That scene is an original concept that owes nothing to anything else. They both happen to be set on London rooftops – that's all. You can't make a Federal case out of that.'

Twinkle stood her ground. 'It's a dead steal,' she accused.

'I will get that other script, and we will go through it line by line and shot by shot. I will prove to you beyond any shadow of a doubt – '

'Steady, Morris,' Dick Brouder advised. 'Don't let her sidetrack you. That's what she's trying to do. The point in question is whether or not she's going to *do* the scene.'

'I'm not,' Twinkle said flatly.

'Equity . . .' Mr Herkimer intoned in the background. He seemed to have appointed himself a one-man Greek chorus: 'Screen Actors' Guild . . . Equity . . .'

'You can't expect Equity to do anything about Twinkle,' Frances protested. 'She's just a child. Surely, Equity wouldn't do anything to her – '

'Don't you believe it,' Mr Herkimer said. 'The youngest actress ever disciplined by Equity was only six years old. She was fined for biting her fellow actors on stage during performances. Twinkle's not too young for Equity to deal with – and she knows it!' He resumed his litany, raising his voice over the increasing tumult. 'Equity . . .'

'Look, Twinkle.' Dick Brouder was holding out a harness of webbed straps. 'Just try it on. See how comfortable it is – ' He sounded like a salesman trying to persuade a reluctant customer. 'See how strong it is. Just try it on. Just for a minute – '

'I won't!' Twinkle backed away. 'You can't make me!'

'Equity . . . Screen Actors' Guild . . . Equity . . .'

'I don't care!' Twinkle flung Mr Herkimer a beleaguered glare. 'You can report me anywhere you want to. I'm not going up there!'

'You're nervous, that's all.' Morris Moskva controlled himself with a visible effort. 'That's understandable. You're just a little girl.'

'I may be little' – Twinkle's mouth tightened – 'but I'm not dumb enough to go up *there*!'

'It's perfectly safe, Twinkle,' Dick Brouder argued. 'Even if you should slip, the safety-harness would stop you before you fell very – '

'Why isn't there a safety-net?' Twinkle interrupted.

'Because the scene isn't dangerous – ' Dick Brouder's voice was rising. 'You are *not* going to fall. The harness will see to that – '

'I don't like the look of that harness,' Twinkle said.

'Nonsense!' Cecile Savoy intervened. 'I wore a harness *just* like that every night in *Peter Pan* – and three matinees a week. I simply relaxed, and gave myself up to it, and *soared* out over the audience like a bird. *And* I was older and heavier then than you are now.'

Twinkle muttered something which was, probably fortunately, inaudible.

'I'll tell you what – ' Morris Moskva offered recklessly. '*I'll* go up there with that harness on! How about that? If I go up there and come down again in that harness, are *you* still going to be chicken about it?'

'That harness would never fit you, Fatso,' Twinkle said.

'It's adjustable,' Dick Brouder said, holding it away as Morris Moskva reached for it. 'But let's not rush into this, Morrie. I'm not sure it's the best idea. I mean, you're at your top weight now and – '

And that was not inconsiderable. Morris Moskva must have been tipping the scales at close to the limit

that they would register. Frances began to share Dick
Brouder's unease.

'What's the matter?' Twinkle jeered. 'I thought you
said it was "*perfectly safe*".' She mimicked Dick Brouder's
tone exactly.

'It is – for *you*.' Dick Brouder glared at her. How did
you convey to a colleague that he was an overgrown ox,
who was likely to endanger his heart, if nothing else, if
he went clambering around on high catwalks designed
for much smaller people?

'*Give* me that!' Morris Moskva snatched the harness
away from him as he hesitated. 'How do I get into this?'
His fingers scrabbled at the buckles and loops.

'Here, let me help,' Ilse Carlsson said. 'It is adjusted
for Twinkle. And, of course, her costume – '

'Will it fit me, or not?' Morris Moskva interrupted.
'That's all I want to know.'

'Yes, of course.' Ilse wrestled with the straps. 'It is
simply a question of readjusting – '

'Great!' Morris Moskva began moving towards the
platform crane that would lift him to the upper level.
'Then let's get going and you can fix it on me up there.'

'Lights!' Dick Brouder ordered, and the rooftops of
Victorian London sprang into glowing life up above
them. He hadn't ordered a camera but, somewhere in
the background, Frances heard one beginning to whirr
quietly.

'Okay, Morrie – ' Dick shouted. 'Let's get this over
with!'

Humming the opening bars of Twinkle's number,
Morris Moskva minced into view. In an ungainly parody
he coyly fluttered from chimney-pot to gable window.

The unknown cameraman had been right to begin shooting. This footage, although unusable in the finished film, would provide after-dinner amusement at Herkimer-Torrington parties for years to come. It would undoubtedly become an 'in-crowd' classic.

> *'Oh, lovely, lovely London,*
> *'How happy I could be . . .'*

Morris Moskva broke into the chorus and moved down towards the edge of the rooftops, still clowning, still giving a wickedly recognizable caricature of Twinkle –

> *'My lovely, lovely London – '*

Suddenly something went wrong and it wasn't funny any more. One foot skidded out from under him and he fought for balance. His arms windmilled wildly, his other foot began to skid –

'Thank God for the harness!' Cecile Savoy said. Fleur-de-lis yapped hysterically.

Morris Moskva plunged downward, as though in parachute harness with no parachute attached. The webbed straps reached the limit of their endurance and stretched taut, suspending him in mid-air, a figure bouncing on an invisible trampoline.

'Wet – !' He shouted indignantly. 'The goddam roof was wet!'

The harness seemed to creak and sigh. Then with a series of popping sounds, like a string of small firecrackers going off, the webbed strands began to part one after another.

Before anyone could move, Morris Moskva continued his downward plunge, ending with a ghastly thump on the floor of the sound stage.

Ilse Carlsson's scream floated down from the catwalk, to be echoed by other screams below. Cecile Savoy fainted.

'You see – ' Twinkle stooped and gathered up Fleur-de-lis. She spoke in a voice of sweet reasonableness, as though talking only to the Peke. She was the calmest of them all.

'You see. I *told* you so.'

CHAPTER XVI

Frances answered the telephone unprepared for the hectoring voice. 'Mother, this is impossible! You must come and stay with us – where you'll be *safe!*'

'Keep calm, dear,' Frances replied, with a blandness she did not feel. It had been quite some time now since she had thought of herself as Mother and, in any case, she was *not* Amanda's mother. 'There's nothing to worry about.'

'Nothing to *worry* about?' Amanda wailed. 'It was on all the newscasts. "Fatal fall on film set." And where have you *been*? Simon and I drove over to get you and bring you back home with us *hours* ago – and you weren't there. We waited nearly two hours before giving up. And I've been ringing you every quarter-hour since. Thank heavens I've got hold of you at last!'

'Yes,' Frances said, with considerably less thankfulness. 'It was kind of you and Simon to think of that, but I'm perfectly all right. I don't see how you could really have expected me to leave my job at a time like this. You should have known it would be a long time before I could get away.'

'Well, you're away now,' Amanda said firmly. 'And you must stay away. They're obviously careless, irresponsible people – and who knows what might happen next?'

Who indeed? But it would not do to encourage Amanda further.

'In any case, Frances,' Amanda shifted back to protest, solicitude having elicited no response; 'You should have thought of *us*. You might at least have telephoned.'

'I'm sorry, dear,' Frances apologized. 'It wasn't easy to get to a telephone.' She did not want to admit that she had never even thought of telephoning Simon and Amanda. Indeed, she realized with a pang of guilt, she had forgotten their existence. Which was permissible, so far as Amanda was concerned, but as for Simon –

'I suppose,' Amanda admitted with a trace of ghoulish glee, 'it *must* have been rather harrowing for a while.'

'Rather,' Frances said repressively.

The minutes until the ambulance had arrived had seemed endless. They had huddled together, trying not to look at the massive heap crumpled awkwardly on the floor. Even before First darted out to fumble for a pulse that had ceased to flutter and moved back shaking his head, it had been horribly obvious that there was nothing any of them could do.

Obviously feeling grateful for something useful he

could do, First had organized a couple of technicians to carry Cecile Savoy to her dressing-room. Twinkle had retained custody of Fleur-de-lis, cuddling the Peke to her like a teddy bear, and no one had had the heart to try to part them.

Laurenda, in a state of semi-collapse, had been taken in hand by Dick Brouder and led off to the waiting car. Frances had urged a reluctant Twinkle along in their wake. Only too obviously, Twinkle had wanted to stay and absorb every gruesome detail.

Ilse Carlsson had frozen up on the catwalk, clinging to the iron railing, her screams floating down to find echoes amongst the hairdressers and make-up girls still on the floor. A tight-lipped Tor Torrington had ascended in the platform crane with Chips, the carpenter, to pry Ilse loose from her precarious perch and bring her back to earth.

As they left the sound stage, Frances had pinpointed a further reason for disquiet. Continuity had not been part of any of the watching groups. Thinking back, Frances had realized that it had been some time since she had last been aware of Continuity's presence. It was possible, of course, that Continuity had simply been feeling ill again with the after-effects of the stomach-pump and had left the set before the accident . . .

'Mother – are you still there?' Amanda sounded harried.

'Yes, dear,' Frances said. 'I was just thinking.'

'Well, *stay* there,' Amanda directed. 'Simon and I will drive over and get you. You can come here for the night – for the rest of the week – '

'What about my job?' Frances asked.

'Oh, well – ' Amanda seemed surprised that she

should even think of such a thing. 'That's all over now
. . . isn't it?'

'Not at all,' Frances said. 'I was hired as chaperone
for Twinkle for the duration of the film. Morris
Moskva's accident was very sad and unfortunate – but
the rest of us will be filming again in the morning.'

'The morning?' Amanda wailed. 'But I thought we'd
have a quiet day together tomorrow. You could sleep
late, and then the Bridge Club is meeting in the afternoon. A nice, soothing game, with a few of my friends –'

While 'Mother' served up all the film gossip piping
hot. Frances began to understand Amanda's sudden
concern for her welfare.

'That's very kind of you, Amanda,' she said. 'Perhaps
another time – after this film assignment has finished.'

'Surely you could take a day or two off,' Amanda
cried. 'After the terrible shock of witnessing – Er, you
did witness it, didn't you?'

'I saw him fall,' Frances said grimly. 'And, really,
Amanda, I don't want to talk about it.'

'You see,' Amanda said triumphantly. 'You *need* a
a day or two to get over the shock –'

'I doubt that anyone else will be taking any time off,'
Frances said. 'And every one of them knew him better
than I did. They'd consider it rather excessive on my
part to take time off – and I wouldn't blame them.'
It might also be construed as a dereliction of duty,
although it was doubtful that Amanda would recognize
such an old-fashioned concept.

'Oh, but, Mother –'

'I'm sorry, dear,' Frances said. 'I can't stand here
talking. I just came home to collect a few things. The
car is waiting outside for me.'

'Car? *What* car?' Amanda snapped suspiciously.

'The company car,' Frances said, adding smugly, 'The Rolls. It's waiting to take me back to the hotel. Twinkle and her mother need me. I'll be staying at the Herkimer-Torrington suite for the next few days.'

'Mother – you can't! Simon – *speak* to her!'

'Goodbye, Amanda.' Frances rang off before her son could come on the line. Fortunately, her case was packed and she picked it up and was closing the front door behind her when she heard the telephone begin to ring again. She had nearly forgotten Amanda – and even Simon – by the time the latch clicked shut.

Frances swiftly unpacked in her assigned room and joined the others in the sitting-room. They were uneasily silent, yet appeared to want to be together rather than retire to their separate rooms. The only attempt to break the stillness had been neither happy nor successful.

'Shall I get something to eat sent up?' Dick Brouder had suggested. 'I could ring Room Service and – '

Too late, he remembered. Inevitably, the thought of food invoked the image of Morris Moskva. If his ghost were to roam, it would surely haunt the kitchens and refrigerators of the Film Unit.

'*No*, thank you,' Laurenda shuddered.

'I'm not hungry,' Twinkle said.

The others did not break their silence, but one could sense their withdrawal in distaste.

'Sorry,' Dick Brouder muttered. 'I didn't think – '

'You never do,' Twinkle said.

'Baby, don't *you* start – ' Laurenda began. It was doubtful that she would have continued, even had

Twinkle's attention not been distracted by the sound of the front door opening and closing. Everyone faced the sitting-room door and waited. A moment later, Mr Herkimer and Mr Torrington came into the room, followed by First.

'Ladies and gentlemen – ' Mr Herkimer faced them gravely. 'I have just one message for you: the show will go on. Morrie would have wanted it that way.'

Laurenda burst into sobs. Dick Brouder put an arm around her and tried to comfort her. Ilse Carlsson leaned back in her chair and closed her eyes. Frances bowed her head – it had been impossible from the start that Morris Moskva could have survived that fall, but medical science just might have been able to do something – and, certainly, Herkimer-Torrington Productions would have spared no expense.

Twinkle eyed them all with impartial loathing. Frances waited, but the expected outburst did not come. For the moment, Twinkle appeared content to remain in the background of the scene, although she was obviously thinking a great many thoughts of her own – bitter thoughts.

And why should they not be bitter? Frances looked around the room. No one was paying any attention at all to Twinkle. No one seemed to remember that it was Twinkle who should have been doing the dance across the rooftops; Twinkle who should have slipped on the wet roof and plunged to the floor below. Twinkle who might even now be lying in hospital dying – or dead.

Twinkle was aware of it. She sat alone in a corner of the room, pale and withdrawn. She seemed to sense that Frances was watching her, for she raised her eyes then and looked steadily at Frances, then glanced away.

Frances crossed the room to stand beside the child. In the spot where her mother ought to be standing. But Laurenda was luxuriating in mild hysterics, thus claiming the concerted attention of everyone, even Mr Herkimer.

'It's terrible, terrible – ' Mr Herkimer patted Laurenda's shoulder absently. 'But the rest of us must carry on. We must make this the best film ever made. In memory of Morris Moskva. It's the least we can do for him. It's *all* we can do for him.'

'It won't bring him back,' Laurenda sniffled. It was impossible to tell whether that was the real reason for her tears. Was she simply one of those people who cried because they felt it was expected of them? Had she really been fond of Morris Moskva? Or was it that she heard the bell tolling – in some inevitable future – for herself? Certainly, she did not appear to connect the accident with Twinkle. She had not glanced in her daughter's direction throughout the proceedings.

'Laurenda, take it easy,' Dick Brouder said gruffly. 'Pull yourself together – you'll be sick if you keep on like this. Try to control yourself, darling. For all our sakes.'

Twinkle stirred restlessly, but still did not utter. Frances looked down at her, but her head was turned away, her face in the shadows.

'But how did it happen?' Ilse Carlsson moaned. 'How *could* it have happened?'

'We're investigating now.' First seemed eager to impress on them his lack of responsibility. 'It should have been perfectly safe up there. The harness should have held – even Morrie's weight, it should have held. Of course, *he* had no business being up there in the first place. Somebody else – and it might never have happened.'

'It wasn't *my* fault!' Twinkle came to life in spirited self-defence. 'I *told* everybody *I* wasn't going up there!'

'That's right,' Frances said. 'You did. You made that very clear.'

And Cecile Savoy had been the one who had originally offered to go up on the rooftops and demonstrate how safe it was. Cecile Savoy – who had once worn a similar safety-harness in *Peter Pan*, who had no fear of heights and every confidence in the apparatus and in her own skill in using it.

But who would wish to harm Cecile Savoy?

The answer came immediately upon the heels of the question. Twinkle would.

Twinkle, who had been antagonistic towards her from the beginning. Twinkle, who had been terrified by the cruel trick played upon her with the altered costume. Twinkle, who would not recognize that she had brought retaliation upon herself by her own cruel trick upon the hapless Fleur-de-lis.

Twinkle, who – perhaps – might not have realized that such a trick could be fatal.

Twinkle, who had – to all intents and purposes – no mother to guide her.

Or was it that Twinkle was impossible to guide? Was Laurenda's attitude towards her daughter not merely indifference, but a tacit admission that Twinkle was beyond control? Was Twinkle one of nature's 'sports' – a maverick, a renegade, who recognized no rules, bowed to no laws? Was Twinkle, in reality, the monster that other members of the Unit had accused her of being?

Frances glanced down to find Twinkle regarding her sombrely. She instantly felt guilty, as though Twinkle might have read her thoughts.

'You were staring at me,' Twinkle said. She looked tiny and defenceless slumped in the big overstuffed chair, her toes not quite touching the ground. She had changed into one of the new smocked tops her mother had bought for her and seemed lost inside it. Surely Laurenda could have found something that fitted better.

'I'm sorry,' Frances apologized. 'I was a million miles away,' she added, not quite truthfully.

'So was I,' Twinkle said. 'Only not a million – just a few thousand. Can't we go back to California now?'

'Not until the picture is finished!' Mr Herkimer had overheard and whirled on them. 'We have everything here now – the sets, the costumes, the musicians, the technicians. We must finish the picture before we leave. It's much better working here.'

'You mean, it's much cheaper here,' Twinkle corrected.

'That too,' Mr Herkimer admitted. 'But mostly, it's better. And, anyway, I'm not sure the police will let us go until after the investigation and inquest, so we might as well keep right on working. It will take our minds off things.'

'Police?' Laurenda sat upright, throwing off Dick Brouder's arm. 'What have the police got to do with this?'

'Routine – ' First said hastily. 'It's just routine in this country. In the case of accident or sudden death, the police have to see that an inquest is held and satisfy themselves as to what happened.'

'But we know what happend,' Laurenda said indignantly. 'We all saw him fall.'

'Then all you have to do is say so when the police ask,' First assured her. 'It's not an Inquisition, or anything like that. It's just a question of form.'

'I want to have an investigation myself,' Mr Herkimer said abruptly. 'Such a thing has never happened before on a picture of mine. I want to know what went wrong. And what was all that poor Morrie was yelling about water just before he hit the ground?'

Laurenda moaned and sank back in her chair.

'Can't you be more careful?' Dick Brouder snapped. 'It's been a hell of a day. Everybody is in a very sensitive mood.'

Ilse gave a faint sob.

'Sorry,' Mr Herkimer backed down hastily. 'You're absolutely right. I'm sorry. Tomorrow will be time enough. We'll look into it then.'

'Chips and Props are helping the police check over the sets now,' said First. 'They'll know if anything is missing or out of place. They're going to come round with their report as soon as they've finished.'

'Fine,' Mr Herkimer said. 'And the police, too, are busy. They've taken away the film of poor Morrie and they're going to develop it in their own laboratories and see if it shows up what happened. Then, when they come back to us, they'll know what questions to ask. Yes, things are moving. That's what I like to see – action! Isn't that right, Tor?' He looked towards his silent partner.

'I'd be happier if they hadn't had to close down the set for the day – ' Tor Torrington broke off as the atmosphere in the room changed and he realized how unfeeling he had sounded. 'But you're right, Herkie, absolutely right.' He looked around at the others. 'I endorse everything Herkie has said.'

'Thank you, Tor.' Mr Herkimer swept a triumphant look around the room. 'I value your faith in my judgement.' He seemed to feel that the whole matter had been settled satisfactorily.

'I always have faith in your judgement,' Tor said hollowly. He, at least, appeared to realize that there might still be difficulties to come.

'We ought to pull out now, don't you think – ?' First weighed in with a judgement of his own. 'Let these ladies get some rest? They've had a rough day.'

'Good idea,' Mr Herkimer approved. 'Come, come – ' He beckoned Dick Brouder. 'We must let them get their beauty sleep.'

'I just want to go over a couple of points with Laurenda,' Dick said. 'I'll meet you down in your suite in a few minutes.'

'I'm not sleepy,' Twinkle said.

'No one asked you!' Laurenda glared at her daughter. 'Frances, put her to bed, please.'

'I can go myself.' Indignation brought Twinkle to her feet and moved her forward a few steps in a reflex action.

'Then go!' It seemed that Laurenda was able to exert some parental authority when she was sufficiently annoyed.

'Come along.' Frances closed in behind Twinkle, cutting off her retreat and herded her towards the doorway.

'No!' At the door, Twinkle balked suddenly. 'I'm

not going until *he* leaves.'

'That's all right,' Tor Torrington said. 'He's coming with us now, aren't you, Dick?' It was an order.

Reluctantly, Dick Brouder abandoned Laurenda and followed Tor out into the foyer. Mr Herkimer paused in the doorway and looked slowly around the room with the air of a general counting his survivors after a heavy battle.

'Ah, well,' he sighed. 'Get a good night's sleep.'

CHAPTER XVII

In the morning, Twinkle ate her breakfast with a dark and brooding mien that gave warning that she was determined to be more difficult than usual. Before the end of the day, she would be insufferable.

When they reached the studio, it became increasingly clear that Twinkle was reserving her deadliest venom for Dick Brouder. She had begun rehearsals without a hint of insubordination, lulling everyone into a false sense of security. It was not until the cameras actually began to turn that the others became aware that she was subtly sabotaging the scene.

'Phew! – look at that.' Beside Frances, First whistled soundlessly. 'She's using the old shifting focus trick – at her age! Believe me, that kid could give the CIA lessons in the Department of Dirty Tricks!'

'I don't understand.' Frances frowned at the scene going on in front of her. It was the same – and yet it wasn't. The cameras had begun to roll on a close-up of Twinkle and Cecile Savoy facing each other. Both had been positioned so that they would occupy equal screen space, as befitted Cecile's status. In fact, the advantage had seemed ever so slightly to be with Cecile Savoy.

Now, however, the whole scene had altered. Twinkle was facing straight into the camera – but all the camera was recording of Cecile Savoy was the back of her head. The advantage was now definitely Twinkle's.

'What happened?' Frances asked, bewildered.

'Cut!' Dick Brouder shouted, 'Cut – Goddamnit!'

Cecile Savoy whirled to face him, livid with fury. 'Did you see that? I must protest – '

'It's all right, Cecile, I saw it,' Dick Brouder said wearily. 'That's why I stopped the scene. Now, we're going to take it again – from the beginning. And, this time, Twinkle, don't get funny.'

'What? What's the matter? What did I do?' Twinkle quivered with righteous indignation.

'You changed position,' Cecile Savoy said.

'I didn't *move*! Look – ' Twinkle gestured towards her feet, still neatly inside the chalk marks set for them. 'I haven't moved an inch. You can see the chalk marks!'

'That's enough, Twinkle,' Dick Brouder said. 'We all know what you've done. Just don't do it again. Now – from the beginning, please.'

'What *did* she do?' Frances asked First quietly. '*I* don't know.'

'She pulled a fast one,' First said. 'You see the way she's standing now, so that both of them have their faces in focus?'

Frances nodded.

'Well, she started out by putting all her weight on to one foot. You can't tell – unless you're watching for it – that an actor has done that. It's one of the oldest and sneakiest tricks in the game. The other mug has his weight evenly distributed on both feet, the way anyone would expect. Then – Look, look, she's doing it again! Just watch her now – '

Now that she had begun to realize what was happening, Frances could see that Twinkle was almost imperceptibly transferring her weight from one foot to the other and leaning backwards slightly. The result was that, without actually moving her feet, she had shifted the focus farther up and to one side while still facing the camera.

But Cecile Savoy had realized what was happening as well. This time, she refused to pivot to keep facing Twinkle. Instead, she did a bit of weight-shifting of her own. Now they both faced into the camera firmly, almost side by side, making a nonsense of lines which should have been spoken to each other.

'CUT!' Dick Brouder glared at both of them, then seemed to regain his calm with a great effort. 'We're all a little overwrought today,' he said mildly. 'Suppose we take a break. Cecile, I'd like to talk to you for a minute. Twinkle, why don't you go back to your dressing-room and have a drink of milk?'

'Why?' Twinkle demanded sharply. 'What have you put in it *this* time?'

The set was suddenly very quiet.

'On second thoughts,' Dick Brouder said, 'I'll talk to you later, Cecile. I think Twinkle and I ought to have a little chat right now.' He turned on his heel and strode off in the direction of Twinkle's dressing-room.

'I'm not going in there alone with *him*.' Twinkle looked after him malignantly.

'Don't be silly,' First said. 'Your mother's in there.

I saw her go in about ten minutes ago – when you began making trouble. I think she went to lie down.'

'So?' The tone was tough, but Twinkle glanced at Frances uncertainly. The message was clear. She did not consider her mother sufficient protection. Especially where Dick Brouder was concerned.

'So hurry up,' First directed. 'You're holding up the whole production – again.'

'We're on our way,' Frances said. She dropped a hand on Twinkle's shoulder, guiding her across the set. Although Twinkle did not speak, Frances sensed a lessening of her tension. The others did not realize that Twinkle was not just being difficult, as usual, but was genuinely frightened. And not without reason.

Laurenda had been lying down and she struggled upright as Frances and Twinkle entered. Dick Brouder stood to one side, frowning thoughtfully. Frances closed the door firmly behind them. This was obviously going to be a scene for private consumption only.

'Baby,' Laurenda said plaintively, 'why do you always have to keep upsetting everybody?'

'All right, Laurenda,' Dick Brouder said. 'I'll handle this. Sit down, Twinkle.'

'I don't want to,' Twinkle said.

'You'd better sit down, Twinkle. This has nothing to do with what happened on the set. Your mother and I have something to tell you.'

'Dick – ' Laurenda began a protest. 'I don't think we ought to. Not right now.'

'She has to know, Laurenda. The longer we put it off, the harder it will be.'

'I don't want to know!' Twinkle clapped her hands over her ears. 'I won't listen! You've got nothing to say

I want to hear!' She shut her eyes tightly and pressed her hands closer over her ears. She seemed to be holding her breath, as well. She began to turn an interesting shade of crimson.

'We all have to do things we don't want to do, Twinkle,' Dick Brouder said patiently. 'And the older we grow, the more we have to.' He glanced at Frances apologetically. 'I'm sorry you had to be dragged into this, Frances. You can leave now, if you like.'

'NO!' Twinkle screamed. Apparently she was not blocking off as much sound as she appeared to be.

'I think perhaps I ought to stay,' Frances said. 'I'm sorry. I don't mean to intrude, but – '

'But she's my chaperone!' Twinkle removed her fingers from her ears and reached out frantically to take a firm hold on Frances's arm. 'She's supposed to take care of me.'

'And you don't think your mother or I will?' The inference was plain.

'*You* won't!' Twinkle glared at him.

'I'm sorry you feel that way, Twinkle, because – '

'NO!' Twinkle turned away, but it seemed to Frances that she already knew what Dick was going to tell her. She was fighting a delaying action against a truth she had no wish to have verified.

'Yes, Twinkle,' Dick Brouder insisted. 'Your mother and I – '

' No! *No!* NO!'

' – are going to get married.'

'NO-o-o-o . . .' It was a long and heartfelt wail.

'Dick,' Laurenda said nervously, 'maybe you'd better leave us alone for a little while now – '

'NO!' Twinkle howled. 'No, you are *not* going to

marry my mother! You can't! I won't let you! You'll marry my mother over my dead body – ' She halted abruptly, seeming to listen to what she had just said.

'Or is that the idea?' she asked, with sudden dangerous quietness.

'Twinkle, I don't know what's going on in your twisted little mind – ' Dick Brouder began.

'I was supposed to drink that milk – ' Twinkle backed away as he showed signs of advancing on her. 'Only Continuity drank it instead, and she nearly died.'

' – but you've got to snap out of it. Come and live in the *real* world, Twinkle, it isn't so bad.'

'And I was supposed to wear that safety-harness – ' Twinkle seemed not to have heard him. 'Only Morrie wore it instead, and he *did* die.'

'Twinkle, you're imagining things.'

'And *you* wanted me to drink the milk – you kept telling me to. And *you* wanted me to wear the flying-harness – you kept promising me it was safe – '

'It *was* safe! Goddammit, Twinkle, you've got to remember that Morris was a full-grown man – and dangerously overweight to begin with. He should have known better. That harness would have held a kid your size. There was no danger – '

'With me out of the way,' Twinkle persisted, 'you wouldn't have had any trouble about marrying my mother, would you? She'd have been a pushover – '

Frances stepped forward quickly as Dick Brouder raised his hand. He let it fall again and twitched his mouth in a strained smile.

'Sorry,' he said. 'But sometimes she gets to be too much for me.' He hesitated. '*You* don't believe any of that nonsense, I hope?'

Frances found that she could not meet his eyes.

'I see.' He shrugged. 'Well, it's your privilege, I suppose. I must admit, she makes out a fairly convincing case.'

'She's crazy,' Laurenda moaned. 'My own daughter and, if I say it myself, she's crazy.'

'Not crazy enough to let you marry *him*!' Twinkle snarled. 'He'd take you for everything you were worth and then disappear. I've seen *his* type around the Studios before this.'

'Believe it or not, Twinkle,' Dick Brouder said, 'I intend to support your mother. Yes, and you, too.'

'We don't need your "support",' Twinkle snapped. 'I make more money than you do!'

'That's true at the moment, Twinkle, but there may come a time – '

'There'll *never* come a time! You're no good! You're a lousy director! I only got stuck with you on this picture because my mother said I had to. If I'd known – '

It struck Frances that, if Dick Brouder *were* a murderer, Twinkle was taking a dangerous risk in antagonizing him like this. It also occurred to her that it was not the safest thing in the world to be a witness to such accusations, either.

'Twinkle, honey, don't get so upset. We'll talk this over tonight and – '

'There's nothing to talk over! The decision is made and Twinkle will just have to accept it.' Dick Brouder spoke with more assurance than he appeared to feel, judging from his anxious glance towards Laurenda. She was so accustomed to letting Twinkle have her own way that it was still possible that she might allow Twinkle to reverse any decision she had made.

Except that Dick Brouder seemed as determined to have his own way as Twinkle was. Frances began to feel a certain sympathy for Laurenda, who might not be so much basically weak as simply exhausted by the warring emotions clashing around her. No wonder she felt the need to lie down so often.

'I *won't* accept it!' Twinkle's voice rose.

'Please, baby, my head is aching.' Laurenda looked as though she wished everyone would go away so that she could lie down again.

'He tried to KILL me!' Twinkle screamed. 'Don't you even *care*? Are you going to marry him so that he can keep on trying?'

'Baby – ' Laurenda put a hand to her forehead and closed her eyes wearily. 'You don't understand – '

'He tried to *kill* me,' Twinkle repeated stubbornly. 'I can understand that.'

But, as Dick Brouder had pointed out himself, the milk had not been lethal. And the safety-harness would most probably have been adequate for a small slim child. Both incidents might have frightened her badly but would not have killed her. Nevertheless, there had been an element of risk in both attempts and, in fact, the last one *had* gone wrong, resulting in Morris Moskva's death. The fact that it had only been intended to terrify a ten-year-old child was not likely to be a strong inducement to any jury to recommend clemency.

'Twinkle,' Dick Brouder said in a defeated voice, 'I don't know what to say. I don't know how to convince you – '

'You can't,' Twinkle said. 'Unless – You can leave! You can go back to California. Right now. And leave me and my mother alone!'

'You know I can't do that, Twinkle. We're in the middle of a film.'

'First can finish it,' Twinkle said. 'He can do it as well as you can. Maybe better.'

'I don't want him to go.' For once, Laurenda found the courage to make a firm statement. 'I love him. I'm going to marry him. If he goes, I go with him!' Then, apparently exhausted by the effort, she sank into the nearest chair and stared at the floor, refusing to meet anyone's eyes.

'You don't mean it!' Twinkle was aghast.

'That's the way it is, Twinkle.' Dick Brouder moved over to stand beside Laurenda, putting his hand on her shoulder. 'When you grow up, you'll understand.'

The silence was broken by a diffident tap on the dressing-room door. Then the door opened and First poked his head inside cautiously.

'Dick,' he said. 'The police are here. They've begun interviewing people about what happened yesterday.'

'That's good,' Twinkle said. 'Because I want to talk to them. There are some things they ought to know.' She gave her mother a malignant look. 'And *then* we'll see who goes anywhere. Except to jail.'

'Don't be silly, Twinkle,' Dick Brouder said wearily. 'You don't really imagine the police would listen to the lies of a nasty spiteful child, do you?'

'They'll listen to the truth,' Twinkle said. 'Even if I *am* a child, they'll have to believe me. Other people can back me up. They all know these things happened.'

'Baby, be sensible,' Laurenda pleaded, raising her head. 'You know Dick was down on the floor with the rest of us when Morrie fell. You can't make anybody believe that he was lurking up on the catwalk with a bucket of water to make poor Morrie slip on.'

'He didn't have to be,' Twinkle said smugly. 'Not when he went up there half an hour earlier carrying a tray of ice cubes!'

CHAPTER XVIII

First took over the Direction while Dick Brouder went to talk to the police. The scene went smoothly, perhaps because Twinkle was too preoccupied with her own thoughts to be difficult.

Would the police bother interviewing a ten-year-old child? And, if they did, how much would they believe of what she told them?

Had Twinkle been lying? Or had she simply been telling the truth as she saw it? Which did not necessarily mean that it bore any relation to reality. Why shouldn't Dick Brouder have been carrying a tray of ice cubes at some point? Everyone had access to the communal fridge and helped themselves freely. People – especially the Americans – were always delving in the fridge for ice cubes for their soft drinks. Dick Brouder was not the only person who might have been roaming around the set with supplies of ice cubes. And, even if they had originally been in his possession, that was not to say that they had remained in his possession. He might have set them down anywhere, after taking a few for his drink, and someone else could have taken the tray and turned the remaining ice cubes into a deadly weapon. If Twinkle had seen Dick Brouder with a tray of ice cubes and later saw someone climbing to the catwalk with a tray of ice cubes, she might have assumed that she was seeing Dick Brouder again. It was a natural mistake.

'Cut! That's fine,' First said, only a trace of surprise in his voice. 'All right, you can all relax for a few minutes while we set the lighting for the next shot.'

Most of the onlookers immediately dispersed, knowing from experience that those 'few minutes' could stretch out indefinitely.

'I'm tired,' Twinkle said. 'I want to go back to my dressing-room and listen to music. I've got a new record.'

'Sure,' First said expansively. 'Why not?' A question he was to regret shortly. 'Go ahead.'

'Call me when you want me,' Twinkle said unnecessarily and walked off.

Frances held a brief wrestling match with her conscience and managed to win, for a change. She remained on set watching technicians rearrange the lighting and keeping an eye out for Continuity, who must surely heave into sight sooner or later. She still wanted to have that talk with Continuity.

'I shall take Fleur-de-lis walkies,' Cecile Savoy announced, managing to invest the statement with a spurious dignity, and stalked over to unloop her pet's leash from around the chair leg. The Peke frisked joyfully around her feet for a moment before making an abortive friendly dart towards the departing Twinkle.

Cecile Savoy pulled so tightly at the leash that she brought Fleur-de-lis up on her hind legs, whimpering and pawing the air with her forepaws, unable to understand why she wasn't allowed to go and play with her dear friend.

Twinkle did not look back, although she must have heard the whimpering. Cecile gave a final tug at the leash and Fleur-de-lis toppled over backwards, then gave the canine equivalent of a shrug and trotted after her mistress. They headed for the outer door of the sound stage and the green fields beyond.

'So far, so good.' First rubbed his hands together uneasily and beamed at Frances. 'It *is* going well, don't you think?'

'Oh, very well,' Frances agreed hastily. She judged it better not to mention her private suspicion that Twinkle was being so good only because she was channelling her main energies into plotting further mischief. It might be a Fool's Paradise, but First had earned his right to it. If her suspicion was correct, his complacency would be shattered rapidly enough.

'That's what I thought.' First allowed satisfaction to creep into his voice. 'Is Dick still in there with the police?' He swivelled his head to look at the closed door of the Production Office and nodded with further satisfaction. The floor was still his for another scene or two.

'Excuse me,' he said to Frances. 'I have to go and check a couple of points with Sparks and Props.' He bustled off happily, an understudy who had been given his chance at the starring role. No matter that the few scenes he directed would be indistinguishable when the entire film was cut and assembled. For the moment, he was a happy man.

Muted, vaguely familiar orchestral strains began to emanate from behind the closed door of Twinkle's dressing-room. Frances could not immediately identify the composition and was unable to discern why it should compound her uneasiness.

Across the set, the office door opened and Dick Brouder came out. He glanced towards Twinkle's dressing-room and hesitated, then walked purposefully in the opposite direction.

Almost immediately, the door of Twinkle's dressing-room opened, releasing a burst of melody and Laurenda who looked around the set, blinking, like someone emerging from a darkened cave. As though by instinct, Laurenda turned and walked off in the direction Dick Brouder had taken.

Laurenda had looked distraught. But then, Frances comforted herself, Laurenda usually did. Or had there been a further scene with Twinkle in the dressing-room? Twinkle was being too good on set – she *must* be reserving her energies for trouble-making elsewhere.

'Right!' First was back at her side, rubbing his hands together briskly. He had missed seeing Dick Brouder finish with the police and did not realize that his precarious authority might be taken from him at any moment. 'Let's get on with the next shot, shall we?' He signalled to the Second Assistant Director, who went scurrying towards the dressing-rooms to assemble the principals.

Uncharacteristically, Twinkle opened her dressing-room door herself to his knock and nodded agreement to his summons. She did not leave her dressing-room, however, nor did she close the door firmly.

Distracted by the partly-opened door, Frances barely noticed that Mr Herkimer had reappeared on set and was standing close to her.

Julian Favely had also appeared. 'Which scene are they going to do?' he asked. 'Everything's turned upside down today and the Call Sheet's useless. Am I supposed to be "on" or not?'

'I don't know – ' Frances began, but Mr Herkimer cut her off.

'You just stand by,' he ordered. 'The police are interviewing and we don't know who they'll want to see next. If it's Cecile, you'll do the scene where Mr Carmichael discovers Sara is his dead partner's lost child – the one he has been looking for in order to share the proceeds of the diamond mine with her, as he promised Captain Crewe. But if the police don't require her, Cecile will do the scene where Miss Minchin discovers that Sara is an heiress after all and that she should have treated the child better. Twinkle's costume is the same in both scenes, so that will be all right.'

'Suppose the police want to talk to Twinkle?' Frances could not refrain from asking.

'What would they want to talk to *her* for?' Mr Herkimer dismissed the idea out of hand. 'Listen, even I wouldn't talk to her if I didn't have to.'

'What about Continuity?' Frances asked. 'I haven't seen her at all today. Where is she?'

'Poor dear girl, she was still not feeling well. I told her to stay home and we would manage without her today.' Mr Herkimer tried to look noble and succeeded in looking shifty.

'But surely the police will want to talk to her. After all – '

'No, no, no!' Mr Herkimer said. 'They must not talk to her. It would only confuse them. What happened to her was an accident. One accident on the set, they could accept – *two* accidents and they would try to make something more out of them. We don't want Continuity dragged into this.'

There was sudden action at the far side of the sound stage. Cecile Savoy had entered and was advancing on to the set, Fleur-de-lis frisking at the end of her leash.

The door of Twinkle's dressing-room quivered and swung farther ajar.

Props darted on set and made some last-minute adjustments to the arrangement of furniture. Somewhere in the background, Sparks must have been busy, for the lights brightened and darkened in strategic spots.

Through it all, nearly everyone on the set must have been keeping a surreptitious eye on the Production Office door watching to see who would be summoned next. Was one of them someone with a guilty conscience?

'Be a good girl,' Mr Herkimer cajoled, 'and don't mention Continuity. Don't even *think* about her!'

Cecile Savoy looped the end of the leash around one leg of her camp chair, gave Fleur-de-lis a final pat, and came towards the others. 'Are we ready to start?' she asked.

'Any minute now,' First assured her. He divided a worried glance between Twinkle's dressing-room and the impatient Cecile. 'You just have time to fix your hair.'

Cecile's hair was not at all disarrayed, but the ruse succeeded. She raised a hand to smooth it unnecessarily. 'Call me when you need me,' she said, and retreated, not noticing the whimpers following her from Fleur-de-lis.

'Where's that kid?' First demanded. 'She said she was coming. All hell will break loose if she keeps Cecile waiting any longer.'

'I'll get her.' Frances hurried towards the dressing-room.

Twinkle was hunched over her hi-fi equipment, making some adjustments to the volume.

'They're waiting for you,' Frances told her.

'Already?' Twinkle straightened up and squared her shoulders, looking more grimly resolute than the simple playing of a scene warranted. 'Tell them I'm coming,' she said. 'I'll only be another minute.'

Frances was halfway across the set to deliver the message before she realized that she had been expertly manipulated out of the room. She halted uneasily, maternal echoes of 'Find out what the children are doing and tell them to stop it' hovering in her mind, and half turned to go back to Twinkle.

As she turned, she caught a movement in the shadows and saw Continuity lurking there. Catching her eye, Continuity put her fingertip to her lips and slid towards the Production Office. Continuity looked around nervously, assuring herself that everyone's attention was still centred on Frances, then tapped on the door and entered abruptly, almost as though she feared pursuit.

Frances was conscious of a sinking feeling in the pit of her stomach. Despite Mr Herkimer's determined optimism, it had been almost inevitable that the police would want to talk to Continuity. It had obviously not occurred to any of them that Continuity would want to talk to the police. And yet, they should have thought of it. Whose life had been endangered? Whose reputation had been impugned?

Frances realized that the others were watching her expectantly and started forward again. 'Twinkle is coming in just a minute,' she reported to First. There was no point in reporting anything else. They would find out soon enough.

'That's fine,' Mr Herkimer nodded approval. 'You're a good influence on her. I knew it as soon as I saw you.' He lowered his voice. 'You could be a good influence on me, too, if you'd only – '

First cleared his throat, reminding Mr Herkimer that he had an audience. Mr Herkimer fell back a step, scowled at his watch, then looked up and across the set and his scowl cleared.

'You see – ' He gestured triumphantly at Twinkle, who was coming towards them. 'A minute! What did I say? A good – a *very* good influence.'

Frances noticed that Twinkle had left her dressing-room door wide open. She tried to fight down the qualm assailing her. There was nothing sinister about an open door. Just because Twinkle had always insisted on having it closed in the past –

'Places, please,' First said. 'We'll just do a quick run-through before we start shooting.'

Obediently, Twinkle and Cecile moved to their chalk marks and faced each other. Faint strains of music sounded in the distance. The others paid no attention. It didn't matter since they weren't actually shooting.

It was a key scene in the film and Frances was not surprised to see that the other actors and technicians were standing on the sidelines to watch. Tor Torrington, perhaps mindful of his budget, had also made one of his rare appearances on set and was standing motionless in the shadows behind one of the lights.

'Right,' First said. 'This is the scene leading up to the number "It Was All for Your Own Good". Miss Minchin, you've just found out – ' He broke off and looked around frowning, having just noticed the music in the background. 'What is this? Someone needs mood music?'

The unseen orchestra built to a crescendo and a chorus of voices suddenly trumpeted: '*There is nothing like a Dame –* '

Cecile Savoy went white with fury.

'Oh God!' Julian Favely moaned. 'And just when she was getting over it and looking forward to the next Honours List!'

Twinkle faced Cecile Savoy, smirking, while the record on her hi-fi continued to blare out the song. There could be no doubt that the insult was calculated and deliberate.

'You brat!' Cecile Savoy took a step forward, hand upraised.

'She's just a child!' Surprising herself, Frances moved forward and caught Cecile's hand on the downward swing just before it struck Twinkle's face.

'Easy, girls, easy.' Somehow, Mr Herkimer was between them and had captured both their hands. 'You've got good reflexes,' he complimented Frances absently, then turned his full attention on Cecile.

'Cecile, darling, you can't hit her now. You hit her, she'll cry, her face will swell up and go all red, her make-up will be ruined, and we won't be able to do any more shooting today. For God's sake, somebody shut off that damned record!' he snapped over his shoulder.

Tor Torrington detached himself silently from the

onlookers and hurried to the dressing-room. The music
stopped abruptly in mid-line.

'That's better,' Mr Herkimer said. 'Now, let's get
back to work. Cecile! Twinkle! No more nonsense!'
He glared at them both sternly, then leaned forward and
pecked Cecile on the cheek. He also murmured something in her ear. It seemed to calm her, even to cheer
her. A faint smile flitted across her lips and she looked
more relaxed as she faced Twinkle and they began the
scene again.

Mr Herkimer had not released Frances's hand. When
she struggled to free it, his grip tightened. 'You
remind me of my third wife,' he murmured. 'She
didn't understand me, either, but she had Class.'

'What did you say to Cecile?' Frances tried a
diversionary tactic. 'She looks a lot happier.'

'She is,' Mr Herkimer said. 'I promised her she
could hit Twinkle later. After we've finished the picture.'

CHAPTER XIX

'That kid is poison.' Tor Torrington came over to
join them. 'This is the last picture we ever make with
her.'

'It probably will be . . . anyway,' Mr Herkimer said.
Tor looked more cheerful, as well.

'PLEASE – ' First shouted. 'QUIET ON THE
SET!'

'He's right. We're out of order.' Tor led them farther
away from the rehearsal.

Frances was relieved to see that the door of the Production Office was still in sight from the corner where they paused. She wanted to see what happened when Continuity came out. She was also beginning to realize that *she* might be next on the list of interviewees. Yet, what could she tell them? She had not actually seen or heard anything that might be considered valid evidence.

'That's it.' Mr Herkimer's attention was still on the scene behind them. 'They've settled down and they're working again. They're nearly ready to shoot.' He met Tor's eyes. 'If we can just keep them at it, we may bring this picture in on target, after all.'

'We may.' Tor did not sound encouraging. He was watching the actors avidly, his gaze concentrated on Twinkle.

Frances had the abrupt, unnerving thought, *if looks could kill . . .*

'What's the matter?' Mr Herkimer was suddenly alert to his partner's preoccupation. 'What's she doing now?'

'It's all right.' Tor relaxed and turned away. 'For a minute, I thought – '

'What? What did you think?' Mr Herkimer stepped towards the actors suspiciously. 'What was she trying now?'

'QUIET!' First shouted again. 'Quiet, *please*. This is a take!'

The clapperboard snapped out its warning and the cameras began whirring.

Uneasily, Frances glanced around the set. Surely Laurenda ought to be somewhere close at hand to watch Twinkle through this key scene, supporting her with silent encouragement from the sidelines.

But Laurenda was not in sight. Neither was Dick Brouder. Presumably they had found each other and were oblivious of the fate of both daughter and film.

To be fair, Twinkle obviously neither needed nor expected outside encouragement. She kept a professional eye on First, responding expertly to any silent instructions he mimed, modifying her performance in accordance with his direction. In fact, she worked more smoothly with him than she had done with Dick Brouder, which was, perhaps, not to be wondered at.

Or was it? Could it be that Twinkle was deliberately trying to give the impression that First was a much better director than Dick Brouder? Certainly, it seemed that she hated Dick Brouder enough to do anything to blacken his name, if not ruin his reputation.

Was the hatred mutual? Despite his guise of tolerant amiability, did Dick Brouder hate her as thoroughly as she hated him? And could he really be blamed if he met hostility with hostility?

In front of the cameras, the scene continued smoothly. Both Twinkle and Cecile Savoy knew what they were doing and did it well. Even Frances could see that they weren't going to need any retakes, although First would probably order one or two just to be on the safe side. If there were any faults, they would be technical.

With a pang, Frances realized abruptly that the picture must be nearly finished. Time had gone so swiftly and the off-screen personality clashes had absorbed so much of her attention that she had not noticed how much of the picture was actually being shot despite the difficulties surrounding the shooting.

There must be very few scenes remaining. And chief

among them must be the rooftop dance. Or would they abandon that now?

Another round of spontaneous applause followed on First's shout, 'Cut!'

'Good,' Mr Herkimer said loudly to his stars. 'Very good. A few more scenes like this one, and we've got ourselves a picture!'

'That's right.' Dick Brouder appeared from the back of the sound stage; Laurenda was with him. 'So let's not waste any more time. We'll shoot the rooftop scene next.'

'We won't,' Twinkle said stubbornly.

'We will.' His stubbornness was as great as her own. 'However, we'll shoot it on the floor, if you like.' He signalled to Sparks, who signalled back and did something with various levers.

The rooftops groaned, squeaked, and began a gradual descent to the ground. They watched in silence until the platform containing the rooftops settled, with a thump and a final groan, on the floor of the studio.

'If it's been able to do that all along –' Twinkle broke the silence – 'Why didn't you put it down here before?'

'Why, indeed?' Dick Brouder's face was grim.

As though on cue, the door of the Production Office opened behind him and Continuity and two of the policemen came out and stood quietly, as though they, too, were interested in the answer to that question.

'It was Producer's orders.' Sparks's voice floated out of the surrounding darkness.

'Never!' Mr Herkimer denied it vehemently. 'Never did I give such an order! I had no idea that set was mobile.'

'Not you,' Sparks said. 'The *other* Producer.'

They wheeled as one to face Tor Torrington. He stood his ground, but the suavity of his smile seemed rather frayed at the edges.

'It was simply a matter of trying to keep expenses down,' Tor said smoothly. 'If we could shoot it at the higher level, we wouldn't have to bother with so many difficult camera shots or expensive trick photography. It makes things easier in the cutting-room, too. It works out at considerably less expense, all things considered – '

'Everything considered except *me*,' Twinkle said bitterly.

'Oh, I took you into my calculations, too,' Tor Torrington assured her. 'The insurance premium on your cover increases quite considerably on your next birthday, you know. And it isn't very far off, is it?'

Amazingly, Twinkle shrank back, instead of flying out in rage at this statement. Frances looked around at the others. Most of them seemed as puzzled as she was, but a few – the inner coterie – obviously knew something that made sense out of Tor's sudden ascendancy over the situation.

'Yes, let's talk about Twinkle's insurance cover, Tor,' Dick Brouder said softly, although he was one of the puzzled ones. 'I noticed it on the Budget back at the beginning of the picture and I thought it was pretty high then. Precisely *what* is she being insured against?'

'Baby – ' Laurenda made a vain effort to change the subject. 'I think you ought to go and rest before the next scene. Dick, don't you want to get the cameras and lights lined up? Herkie – ' recklessly, she appealed to the highest authority she knew – 'make them stop it!'

But there was a quiet reshuffling of places in the background as the police moved forward to stand just beyond the brightly lit group in the centre of the scene. Mr Herkimer was no longer the highest authority available.

Dick Brouder repeated the question. 'What is she being insured against?'

'Nature. An act of God. The march of time – ' Tor Torrington shrugged. 'Whatever you want to call it. She's at a . . . delicate age, and we have our investment to protect. If she should suddenly start to grow . . . in any direction . . . before the picture is safely in the can – ' He shrugged again.

'That's silly! Plain silly!' Laurenda seemed determined on a last-ditch fight. 'I've told you so!' She glanced obliquely at Dick Brouder. 'A ten-year-old child – '

'Don't be a Goddamned fool!' Twinkle caught the glance and her last fragment of control gave way. 'I'm *fourteen* years old!' She gave Dick Brouder an oblique glance of her own. 'We're *both* older than you think!'

Suddenly, it all made sense. Frances remembered the shapeless smocked blouses, the outbursts of hysterical resentment at any reference to ageing or growing up. The refusal to work with other children – real children – on the set. Laurenda's insistence on calling her daughter 'Baby' was more of a reminder than an endearment.

Even the curious smirk on the face of the Immigration official that first day when he turned back for another look at Twinkle's passport was explained. She had thought that he had smiled because Mr Herkimer had denied that Twinkle had a surname – but Mr Herkimer had also just announced that Twinkle was a ten-year-old child. And the year of Twinkle's birth was stamped in her passport as well as her real name.

'So what?' Dick Brouder was unimpressed. If Twinkle had expected her revelation to have any effect on his feelings for her mother, she had thrown down her trump card in vain.

'You shouldn't have said that, baby.' Laurenda was the most upset. 'Baby, you should never – She doesn't know what she's saying – ' Laurenda appealed to the others. 'She's too upset. I hope I can count on all of you never to mention it again. Especially to the Press – '

Mr Herkimer was shaking his head sadly, already aware that such a plea was useless. Twinkle's peculiar vulnerability was the key to the whole situation. So much so that it could not be concealed when the case came to court. Twinkle's days as a child star were over.

'You intended to protect your investment, all right,' Dick Brouder said. 'Twinkle was grossly over-insured. And the picture was nearly finished. It was obvious that nothing drastic was going to happen. Any minor physical changes that might begin now could be disguised for the few shots remaining. You were going to have your picture, but you were greedy enough to want the insurance money, too.'

'That's nonsense,' Tor Torrington said. 'As you've just pointed out yourself, the picture is nearly finished.'

'But the insurance company wouldn't know that, would they? It's a bit out of their line. You could wait a suitable length of time before releasing it and claim that a lot of the scenes had been re-shot or faked using the insurance money – '

'It would have worked,' Mr Herkimer nodded sadly. 'It almost *did* work.'

'He tried to kill me,' Twinkle gasped. '*He* tried to kill me!'

'He didn't mean to kill you, I think.' Mr Herkimer patted her on the head absently. 'He only meant to damage you a little. That would have done just as well for the insurance. There was also an accident clause in the policy. A broken leg or two would have delayed the picture enough for us to collect on not bringing it in on time and all the overtime we'd have had to pay.' His voice was regretful. 'We could have cleared a nice profit.'

'You're trying to claim that Tor did this all on his own?' Perhaps for the sake of the watching police, Dick Brouder tried to get everything as clear as possible. 'You mean you didn't know anything about it?'

'I swear I didn't! I can forgive you anything – ' Mr Herkimer faced his partner and sighed heavily – 'Anything except poor Morris. Why did you have to kill the best scriptwriter we ever had?'

'It was an accident.' Tor Torrington surrendered gracefully. Why shouldn't he? With luck, and the most expensive lawyers, he would receive the lightest sentence on the lesser charge. 'You know it was an accident. Morrie insisted on going up in that harness – '

'That harness was tampered with!' Continuity stepped forward. 'It was all right when Props and I collected it. But it had been deliberately frayed so that it wouldn't hold. The police have found – '

'Even so, it would probably have held Twinkle.' Tor Torrington tried to gloss over the weakest point in his defence. 'She would just have been very frightened – with luck, into a nervous breakdown. We could have collected on that, too. At worst, she'd only have broken a few bones. Even at her advancing age, bones mend easily.'

Frances wondered what the note-taking police really thought. Tor Torrington seemed to be working on his defence even as he confessed, growing more innocent-sounding by the minute. He had talked his way from a murder charge to a manslaughter charge, and now seemed intent on further reducing his culpability. Was there such a charge as malicious mischief? Or perhaps he was trying for mere vandalism?

'Believe me, Herkie, I can't forgive myself, either. If only Morrie hadn't been so determined to go up on those rooftops. How could I have known he'd pull a stupid trick like that? If only he'd ever stuck to one of his diets, it might not have been so bad – '

Now, it appeared, it was all Morris's fault. Next, Tor Torrington would be arguing that it had really been an obscure form of suicide.

'What about the milk?' Continuity demanded. 'That nearly killed *me* – so how much did you put in it?'

'You must have been abnormally sensitive to the stuff,' Tor told her. 'There wasn't enough to hurt the kid, just enough to knock her out for a while. I thought, if she had what seemed to be fainting fits, we could get a doctor over here to sign a certificate of illness and we could collect on that.'

'You louse!' Laurenda had begun shaking violently. 'You rotten louse!'

'Please, Laurenda,' Tor winced. 'Let me explain my position – '

'Suppose you explain it to us, sir.' Two policemen came out of the shadows. 'Down at the Station. It is my duty to warn you . . .'

'Don't say anything else, Tor' Mr Herkimer's voice was anguished. 'Keep your mouth shut until I can get us a lawyer –'

'You needn't worry,' Tor Torrington said. 'I've stopped talking now until my lawyer arrives.'

'Wait a minute!' Mr Herkimer was galvanized into action as the policemen led Tor Torrington away. He raced after them. 'Wait a minute! I'm coming with you! . . .' His voice faded into the distance.

The other actors and the technicians began to melt away, awkward and embarrassed, momentarily unable to cope with a situation for which they had no script, no instructions.

'Come on, Laurenda,' Dick Brouder said gently. 'We'll get you something for that headache now.' He led her off.

Up at the control panel, Sparks was dousing the lights, one by one. Twinkle stood alone in the glow of the last spotlight, arms crossed defensively in front of her, staring down at her feet as though she could see the broken shards of her career there. Then that spotlight, too, dimmed and went out.

CHAPTER XX

'Why don't you go and change?' Frances suggested as she shepherded Twinkle into the empty suite. She had not dared to suggest that Twinkle change out of her costume before they left the studio, feeling that the sooner Twinkle was removed from the scene of so much unpleasantness, the better. They had had to return by public transport since someone – Mr Herkimer, perhaps not allowed to travel in the police car with his partner, or Dick and Laurenda – had commandeered the company limousine. She was thankful that styles were so elastic these days that Twinkle's costume had elicited no more than an occasional smile.

Silently, Twinkle went to her room. Frances remained in the sitting-room. Although Twinkle would no longer protest at being helped to disrobe, now that her secret was out and it no longer mattered if anyone noticed that her shape was changing, there was a new reason for leaving her alone now. Twinkle needed some privacy in which to face her own thoughts in her own way.

Twinkle returned eventually wearing a sweater and skirt. She looked, for the first time, like a young lady growing up. It was the thoughtful expression on her face as much as the dash of lipstick that added to that impression.

'What are you doing to do?' Frances asked.

'I'll go into Summer Stock.' Twinkle did not pretend to misunderstand. 'That's why I was always so careful not to get into any trouble with Equity, even when I was acting most like a kid. I'm still a member in good standing.' Frances realized that she had been thinking about the impending problem for longer than anyone had suspected.

'I don't suppose Broadway would have anything for me – I'm at the awkward age for scripts. But I could do a few seasons on the Straw Hat circuit with one of the classic teenage scripts updated. I'm good enough to keep the customers happy, and maybe I can learn more about acting from the stage angle.'

'That's not a bad idea,' Frances approved.

'I'm going to buy myself a Pekinese, too.' Twinkle revealed another recent decision. 'Just like little Fleur.'

'A *very* good idea,' Frances said. 'I'm sure Cecile will give you the name of the breeder she bought Fleur from.'

'Do you think she would?' Twinkle showed a brief flash of animation before lapsing back into her career problems. 'Of course, I'd rather keep on making films but – '

'The awkward age is even more awkward in front of a camera?' Frances remembered Mr Herkimer's gloating as he contemplated the eventual come-uppance of Twinkle.

'You've heard them talking,' Twinkle said. 'The transition is the hardest one there is, and nobody's going to break their necks trying to find special scripts for me. The kind I need. I guess,' she admitted, 'I've made a lot of enemies.'

'Not enemies,' Frances protested. 'That's too strong a word. You're still almost a child. But I'm afraid you *have* annoyed a lot of people.'

'And always the most important people,' Twinkle sighed. 'Maybe it serves me right.'

Before Frances could find anything comforting to say, they heard the key turn in the front lock, a babble of voices, a rush of footsteps and, abruptly, the sitting-room was crowded with people, all talking at once.

'We'll finish the picture,' Dick Brouder said decisively. 'That's the first item on the agenda.'

'We've got to get the best lawyer in town,' Mr Herkimer dictated. 'Until we can fly our own lawyers over from Los Angeles. And then we've got to – '

'As soon as the picture is finished, I want Twinkle to take a nice long rest,' Laurenda said.

'I shall help in any way I can,' Cecile Savoy declared. Fleur-de-lis yelped encouragement from her arms.

'We'll start shooting again in the morning – '

'Is it too late to call the American Embassy? What time do they stop working? Tell them this is an A-1 priority emergency – '

They continued talking, each embroidering his or her own theme. They ignored Twinkle, even when the conversation seemed to be about her. They were courtiers in a dissolving Court. *The Queen is dead; long live* – who? Suddenly, Frances recognized the parallel she had been searching for since becoming part of the Unit.

'Lady Jane Grey!' she said. The poor forlorn little teenager pushed upon a throne she did not want, forced to accept a crown she had no right to, badly-advised, manipulated, schemed for and schemed against, used to further the ambitions of the power-hungry courtiers surrounding her . . .

'What's that?' They all stopped talking abruptly. Mr Herkimer advanced, almost on tiptoe, as though afraid of startling her. 'What's that, darling? Say it again. Tell Herkie.'

'I – I only said – ' Frances looked around, unnerved at being the centre of so much attention. 'I was just thinking aloud – Well, Twinkle *is* like Lady Jane Grey. A little.'

'A little.' Mr Herkimer turned his gaze to Twinkle, still sitting quietly on the sofa. 'A lady soon, yes. And Lady Jane Grey? It's all coming back to me, but somebody refresh my memory. I think our Frances has just been brilliant!' He beamed fondly at her.

'Lady Jane Grey – ' Cecile Savoy took the floor – 'was a child bride and a child queen. She was only seventeen when her relatives put her on the Throne of England – briefly. She was called the Nine Day Queen, because she was deposed after reigning for only nine days. She was tried for treason and beheaded on Tower Green.' Cecile eyed Twinkle assessingly. 'It could be a highly dramatic, tragic part, with many excellent supporting roles. *I*, of course, have already played nearly every major female role in the House of Tudor.'

'Nobody's done a historical picture in a long while,' Mr Herkimer said thoughtfully. 'It could be time for one to go over big again. It would have Class.'

'The costumes!' Ilse breathed rapturously. 'The brocades, the velvets, the ruffs, the farthingales – '

'We've got a great Unit all set up here,' Dick Brouder said. 'We could put them on retainers while we finish the current picture and cut and dub it. We'll have to come back to England for the trial, anyway. Most of us will be needed to testify.'

'Do you hear them, honey?' Laurenda enthused. 'They've found it! They've found a transition picture for you. After that, you could go on to adult parts.'

'And she dies in the end?' Mr Herkimer's eyes gleamed appreciatively. 'Beheaded? That would fit in with the horror craze these days. We could get a shot of her head rolling towards the audience, spurting blood – '

'I could play that part,' Twinkle said thoughtfully. 'It would give me the chance to do some real acting.

And if I died like that in the end, then everybody would forgive me, wouldn't they?'

'I believe they would,' Frances agreed. Such a death would be symbolic, an atonement and a reparation. And, in a curious way, it would be understood as such by the others in Twinkle's world. They moved among shadows, living for the shadows they created up on a silver screen, shadows that were more real to them than their own lives. And who was to say they were not right? The shadows on the screen would live and love and laugh and talk and play out their scripted destinies long after their creators had aged and died. The shadows were their immortality.

In such a world, Twinkle's symbolic death by the headsman's axe would be understood, accepted – even applauded. From it, Twinkle would arise and go on to fresh triumphs as a young adult star.

'But we need the best scriptwriter available,' Mr Herkimer said. 'The very best. Goddam Tor – we *need* Morris Moskva!'

'Really, Mother,' Amanda said. 'We *do* think you're being unreasonable, don't we, Simon?'

'Not really,' Simon declined to back her. 'If Mother doesn't want to – '

'It's not that I don't *want* to,' Frances lied, in the interests of maintaining an amicable relationship with her daughter-in-law. The days when she had wished to be invited to Amanda's dinner-parties seemed almost beyond recall. She now felt that they would be as dull as . . . as Amanda herself.

'I honestly wouldn't be able to contribute anything to a dinner-party, dear,' she said, letting Amanda know that she realized that she would be expected to be the star turn. 'We aren't supposed to talk about the case until it comes to trial. We've been warned about that.'

'You always have some excuse,' Amanda wailed. 'It all happened *months* ago. And by the time it comes to trial, you'll be working again on the next production. You said so yourself.'

'Well, yes,' Frances admitted complacently. She didn't feel that she ought to admit how much she was looking forward to it.

'I don't see why you can't.' Amanda looked around mistrustfully. Ever since the Unit had returned to California, her mother-in-law's home had been suspiciously full of hothouse roses, citrus fruits and various exotic American delicacies. (Mr Herkimer did not give up easily. And Frances was not absolutely certain that she wanted him to.)

'Excuse me, dear.' Frances dodged round her plaintive daughter-in-law as the telephone rang. She was delighted to hear the voice at the other end.

'Good evening, *Dame* Cecile.' She felt Amanda snap to attention behind her. 'I was so pleased to see your name in the Honours List – '

'Thank you for your sweet note,' Dame Cecile said regally. 'Please *do* continue calling me Cecile. *Such* a bore, all this Honours nonsense, but one must accept it on behalf of the Profession, however little it means to one personally.'

'I understand,' Frances murmured.

'My niece,' Dame Cecile continued, 'Julian's younger sister, is rather high-strung. She must fly back to her Swiss finishing school the day after tomorrow, and we thought it better if she had a *companion* for the journey.'

I remembered how marvellous you were with Twinkle
and – '

'I suppose I *could*,' Frances said, trying not to sound
too thankful. There was probably a hidden snag, but at
least it would mean escape from Amanda's relentless
dinner-party. 'By the way, did you get a wedding
photograph? Didn't Twinkle make a charming brides-
maid?'

'Charming,' Dame Cecile said frostily. Her voice
warmed. '*I* shall be playing her mother, the Duchess of
Suffolk, in the new production.'

'I'm so glad,' Frances said, adding hastily, 'You'll be
marvellous in the role.'

'She *is* one of the Tudor ladies I've never essayed
before,' Dame Cecile said modestly. 'However, I must
tell you that I was mentioning you to a friend and she
wondered if, after you've delivered Juliet to her
finishing school, you might do an errand for her? It
would just be a matter of popping down to Rome and
collecting her eight-year-old son from his father and
bringing him back to London with you – as you'd be
over on the Continent already.'

'I suppose I could . . .'

'Splendid! Meet me for lunch tomorrow and I'll give
you your tickets and expenses money. Of course, you
understand, no expense is to be spared. If you need more
at any time, you're to wire for it – '

'Lunch tomorrow, Dame Cecile.' Frances spoke
loudly and clearly for the benefit of Amanda. 'I'll look
forward to it.'

She listened to Cecile Savoy's parting instructions as
to time and place. Part of her mind was busy tasting and
testing the new realization that had just been borne

upon her. Whatever happened eventually with Mr Herkimer, she would not be discarded and forgotten after the next film. She had been gathered into the theatrical world and was now enmeshed in it, part of it, from now on. She replaced the receiver and turned to face her son and daughter-in-law.

'I'm *so* sorry, darlings,' she lilted. 'But the dinner party is *definitely* out. I've just been called on a new assignment . . .'